A KILLING AT SMUGGLERS COVE

AN IRIS WOODMORE MYSTERY

MICHELLE SALTER

B

Boldwood

First published in Great Britain in 2023 by Boldwood Books Ltd.

Copyright © Michelle Salter, 2023

Cover Design by Rachel Lawston

Cover Illustration: Rachel Lawston

The moral right of Michelle Salter to be identified as the author of this work has been asserted in accordance with the Copyright, Designs and Patents Act 1988.

All rights reserved. No part of this book may be reproduced in any form or by any electronic or mechanical means, including information storage and retrieval systems, without written permission from the author, except for the use of brief quotations in a book review.

This book is a work of fiction and, except in the case of historical fact, any resemblance to actual persons, living or dead, is purely coincidental.

Every effort has been made to obtain the necessary permissions with reference to copyright material, both illustrative and quoted. We apologise for any omissions in this respect and will be pleased to make the appropriate acknowledgements in any future edition.

A CIP catalogue record for this book is available from the British Library.

Paperback ISBN 978-1-83751-068-9

Large Print ISBN 978-1-83751-069-6

Hardback ISBN 978-1-83751-067-2

Ebook ISBN 978-1-83751-070-2

Kindle ISBN 978-1-83751-071-9

Audio CD ISBN 978-1-83751-062-7

MP3 CD ISBN 978-1-83751-063-4

Digital audio download ISBN 978-1-83751-065-8

Boldwood Books Ltd
23 Bowerdean Street
London SW6 3TN
www.boldwoodbooks.com

For my Devonshire ancestors

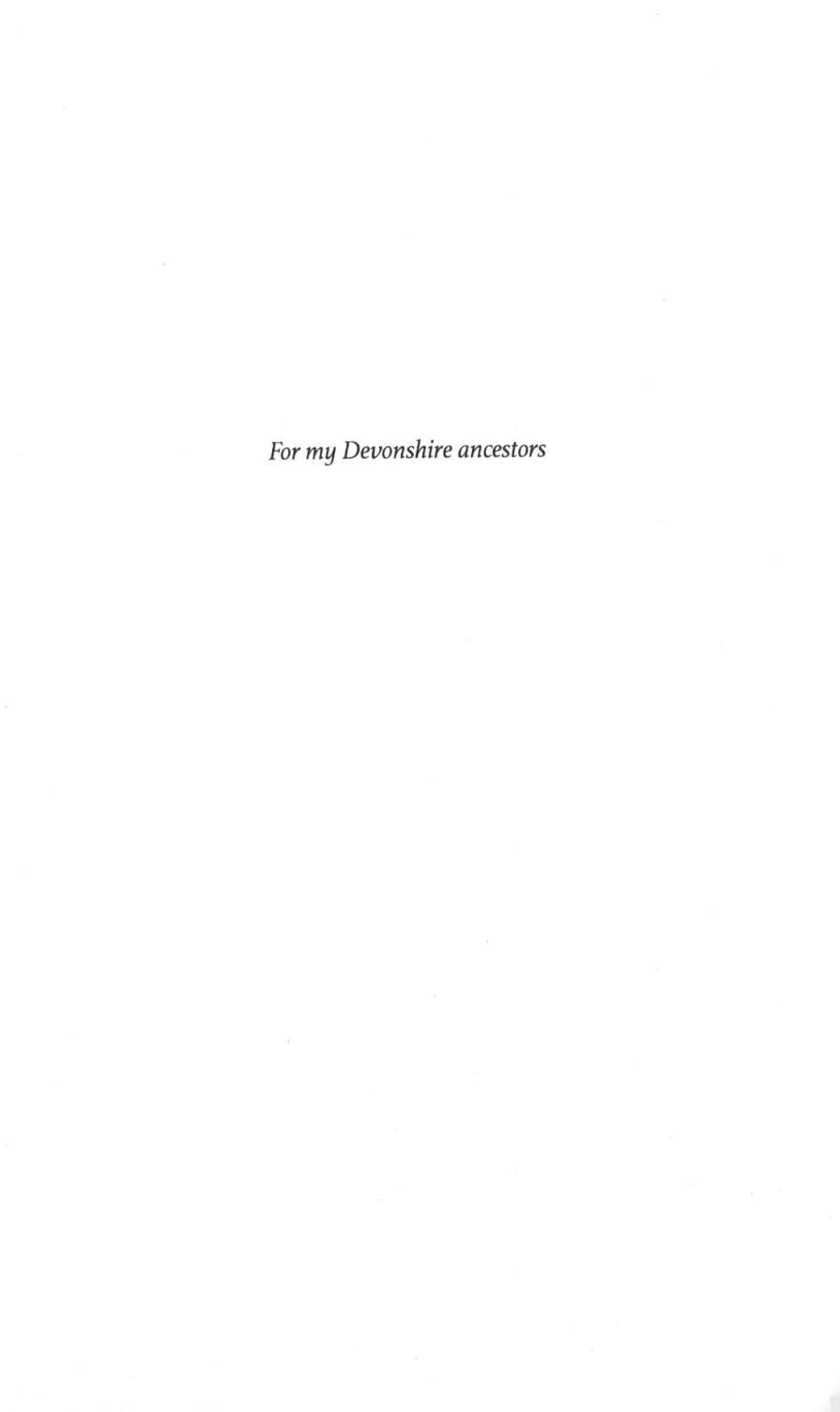

1

1923

Walden

'Millicent's coming to the wedding.'

'That should stop you from getting into trouble.' My boss, Elijah Whittle, lit a cigarette and tossed the match into an ashtray.

'And Percy.'

He took a long drag. 'I take that back.'

'Katherine invited them to please me.' I knew I sounded far from pleased.

'What does the woman have to do to make you happy?'

'She doesn't have to do anything.'

'Just not marry your father?' He sank back and stretched out his legs, resigned to the interruption.

I'd decided it was time for a break, and after placing a cup of coffee on his desk, I flopped into the nearest chair. Since Miss Vale, his assistant, had moved downstairs to the more spacious offices of Laffaye Printworks, it was just the two of us upstairs. I was the only permanent reporter working for *The Walden Herald*, and Elijah kept an eye on me from his smoke-filled den. He'd strategically placed his chair so that he had a clear view of the main office. From this position, he could see my desk, the large railway clock on the wall and anyone coming or going.

'Iris,' he said in exasperation, 'talk to your father. About your mother.'

I shook my head. 'He's the one that doesn't talk about her.'

'He doesn't know what to say because he doesn't know how you feel.'

The problem was I didn't know how I felt. In principle, I didn't mind my father marrying again. I wanted him to be happy. And I liked Katherine. Sort of. I couldn't deny it had been kind of her to invite my friends, Millicent Nightingale and Percy Baverstock, to the wedding.

Elijah scrutinised me through a haze of smoke. 'You're angry.'

'No, I'm not.'

It was true. Most of the anger I'd felt after my mother's death had burnt itself out. But I had to admit, a flicker of resentment remained over the fatal suffragette protest that had robbed me of her shortly before my fifteenth birthday. That had been nine years ago. And it certainly hadn't been my future stepmother's fault. It was just that memories were starting to fade. With my father about to embark on a new life with another woman, I felt like I was losing the remaining precious ties I had to my mother.

'I know this is hard. But...' He eyed me cautiously. 'You need to make more of an effort towards Katherine for your father's sake. He's upset you're planning to move out.'

I changed the subject. 'When are you driving to Devon? Millicent and I are going down by train on Friday the sixth of July.'

The wedding was being held on Saturday, 28 July in the

seaside resort of Dawlish. As it was generally a quiet month for the newspaper, Elijah and I had decided to close the office for a few weeks and make a holiday of it.

'A few days later. I need to sort out the July editions with Miss Vale.' The redoubtable Miss Vale and the rest of the newspaper's staff would be taking care of things in our absence – directed by Elijah from a distance. 'Horace has booked us into the Rougemont Hotel in Exeter.'

It was an expensive hotel with every modern convenience. But then, Horace Laffaye, owner of *The Walden Herald*, was a wealthy man. He'd been in banking. Of a kind. Not your run-of-the-mill retired bank manager, as the people of Walden had first thought when he'd moved to the town. Horace had traded on Wall Street. And he was extremely well travelled. If you named a country, he'd have a story to tell about his time there.

'Percy has a room in a boarding house in Dawlish, and Millicent and I are staying with my grandparents in Exeter. Father will join us there later, and Katherine plans to stay with her brother in Dawlish.' My grandparents were unaware that Katherine often stayed in Walden under the same roof as my father. The social proprieties that the happy couple had so far ignored would be observed once we were in Devon.

'Horace wants us to spend a few days in Dawlish. He thinks the sea air will do me good.' Elijah puffed on his cigarette. 'If that wasn't bad enough, he thinks we should swim in the sea.' He shuddered.

I choked on my coffee at the thought of Elijah in a bathing suit. Could you swim with a cigarette in your mouth, I wondered?

'I'm sure Percy would love to join you for a dip.'

He groaned in response.

'Have you written your speech yet?' I asked.

This prompted an even louder groan. 'What possessed me? I don't like speeches and I don't like holidays.'

Although Elijah had been touched when my father had asked him to be his best man, I knew he didn't want the role but had been too polite to say so. I was counting my blessings that Katherine had decided against having bridesmaids.

To make matters worse for Elijah, Horace, his partner in more than just business, had leapt at the opportunity for them to take a holiday together. Elijah wasn't good at leisurely pursuits. He didn't know what to do with himself if he wasn't working.

Besides, they had to be careful. Theirs was a relationship that could never be made public. It would be strictly two gentlemen friends enjoying a short break while they attended the wedding of a dear friend.

* * *

'Have you invited any of your Dutch relatives?' my father asked Katherine, who seemed to have become a permanent fixture at our dinner table. He thought that with Lizzy, our housekeeper, and me at home, it was entirely respectable for Katherine to stay overnight. Judging by the twitching curtains, the other residents of Chestnut Avenue thought differently.

'It's too far for them to come. And I'd have to help arrange accommodation,' Katherine replied. 'I want to keep things simple.'

Simple? The wedding arrangements seemed to become more complicated by the day and the guest list longer. This was the first I'd heard of a Dutch side of the family.

My surprise must have shown. 'My mother was Dutch,' Katherine explained.

I realised how little I knew about her and that it was probably my fault. I was aware her first husband, Major Laurence Keats, had died during the war. He'd been in the intelligence corps with Father and Elijah. When they were given leave to see Katherine to offer their condolences, my father had discovered she was the younger sister of an old school friend of his, Stephen Damerell.

'Has Elijah prepared his speech?' Father asked.

'He's working on it,' I replied untruthfully.

'I'd like to buy you a new dress,' Katherine said. 'Let's go shopping in Exeter. I know you probably haven't had time to look yet.'

Her innocent smile didn't fool me. She knew I'd given no thought to what I was going to wear for the occasion and wanted to make sure I didn't let the side down.

I took a sip of water and tried to think of some way out of this. 'You don't have to do that. You'll be far too busy with preparations.' It was the best I could come up with.

'It will be fun to spend the day together.'

Thank goodness she refrained from saying 'like mother and daughter'. She had more sense than that.

Aware of my father's anxious eyes on me, I forced a smile. 'Thank you. It's very kind of you.'

Feeling I'd fulfilled Elijah's plea to 'make more of an effort' towards Katherine, I let my thoughts drift, only listening with half an ear to the conversation.

But when Katherine mentioned she'd invited some friends to the reception whom she hadn't seen since her first husband's funeral in January 1919, my attention was drawn back.

'I thought Major Keats died during the war?'

'Shortly after,' Katherine replied.

My father shot me a strange look which I couldn't quite decipher, then went back to discussing the guest list.

I tried to recall exactly what he'd told me when I'd asked him where, and when, he'd met Katherine. I was sure he'd said Major

Keats had been killed during the war and that calling on Katherine to offer his condolences had put him back in touch with Stephen Damerell.

Yet we'd lived in London until October 1919, and whenever Father visited Devon, he'd taken me with him to see my grandparents. Or so I'd thought.

I could hardly probe Katherine about her first husband's death. But something didn't add up about my father's account of when he and Katherine had met.

2

If Katherine wondered what her future husband would be like in twenty-five years' time, she need look no further than my grandfather, Bartholomew Woodmore. In his seventy-fourth year, he was as upright and commanding as he'd been when he was a master at Ladysmith Boys School in Exeter.

My grandmother, Clementina, barely came up to his shoulder. At that moment, she was hugging Millicent.

'Bartholomew can't wait to hear about your school. And I want to hear all about your great aunt. She sounds quite a character.'

Millicent's Great Aunt Ursula was indeed a character. She'd travelled widely, never married, but had more than her share of lovers – if her wilder tales were to be believed. I wasn't sure these stories were suitable for my grandmother's ears, though I knew I could count on Millicent's discretion. As a teacher at Walden's Elementary School, she had a reputation to uphold.

Nan and Gramps didn't know I planned to take lodgings with Millicent and Ursula. To appease my father, I'd agreed we'd discuss it again after the wedding. But my mind was made up.

Father had been absent for much of the war, and afterwards his work as a freelance journalist had taken him abroad for long periods. This meant I'd enjoyed a great deal of independence since my teens and, at the age of twenty-four, I wasn't prepared to lose it. It was troublesome enough having one parent at home, let alone two.

In the afternoon, Millicent and I left my grandparents' townhouse on Bedford Circus, a road of two crescents of elegant Georgian houses that formed a circle. It was in the city centre, close to the cathedral and a fifteen-minute walk to Exeter St David's railway station from where we could catch a train to the seaside town of Dawlish.

I'd made this journey many times over the years and it never failed to astonish me. It was one of the most scenic stretches of railway in Britain. Built to the designs of Isambard Kingdom Brunel, its route from Exeter followed the River Exe to Dawlish Warren, then on to Dawlish, after which it ran beneath sea cliffs to Teignmouth before following the River Teign to Newton Abbot.

The view to the left across the estuary to Exmouth always lifted my spirits. And as the train rolled through Starcross station, we were rewarded by the sight of a seal basking in the sunshine on one of the sandbanks.

Millicent was in raptures. 'I know I'm excited, but I haven't had a holiday in years.'

This was true of many people in the country. It may have been five years since the war ended, but money was still short, and luxuries like holidays were out of reach for most working people.

I couldn't help thinking that Millicent wasn't exactly dressed for a day at the seaside. She looked more like she was on an archaeological expedition, in a full-length skirt, stout shoes and a hefty brown leather bag slung over her shoulder.

For me, the first glimpse of the sea took me back to my adventures of the previous year, travelling through Europe. It hadn't exactly been a holiday. More an escape from a sad situation. An impetuous flight with a man I thought I was in love with. But not married to. When our adventure came spluttering to an end, I returned home in disgrace.

Like a pair of indulgent uncles, Elijah and Horace had let me resume my old job at *The Walden Herald* without too many recriminations. I'd attempted to mend relations with my father, though with Mrs Katherine Keats' arrival on the scene, that hadn't gone as smoothly.

I pushed all thoughts of the impending nuptials, and the mystery of when exactly the happy couple had met, from my mind and sank back into the carriage seat. It was three weeks until the wedding and a lot could happen in that time.

Smoke from the engine billowed past the train windows as we sped through Dawlish Warren station. The view opened up of the sea on one side and red sandstone cliffs on the other.

The train slowed and the whistle sounded as we entered dear old Dawlish. I had so many happy memories of visits to the town when I was a child. My grandparents had taken me there to play on the beach, ride donkeys and eat ice cream.

We emerged from the railway station to find Percy waiting for us. Unlike Millicent, he looked every inch the holidaymaker in his short-sleeved white shirt and new wide-legged blue flannel trousers. Unfortunately, the trousers weren't the only thing that was new.

'What on earth is that?' I stared in horror at the facial hair on his upper lip.

He flushed, looking hurt. 'It's a moustache. I think it rather suits me.'

'It reminds me of Douglas Fairbanks,' Millicent said, ever the peacemaker.

I groaned. He'd never shave it off if he thought it made him look like his matinée idol.

He stroked it, appearing pleased with himself. 'What a lark. I haven't had a holiday since before the war. Isn't this place divine? I'd forgotten what a beautiful stretch of coastline this is.'

If Millicent was in high spirits, it was nothing compared to Percy's excitement. 'What shall we do first? They sell ices over there covered in clotted cream. Oh, and you must come and see the black swans.'

'Let's walk along the beach.' Millicent opened the bag she was carrying. 'I want to take some rock samples to show my class.'

Percy peered inside the bulky leather bag. 'Good Lord, woman. Are you allowed to carry those weapons?' He pulled out a small hammer and chisel. 'The suffragettes used to smash the windows of the department stores on Oxford Street with these.'

I smiled. The same thought had crossed my mind.

We strolled down to the seafront, where the beach was filled with young children building sandcastles. Mothers watched them from beneath brightly coloured parasols.

'Let's go to Coryton Cove.' I pointed to where the railway line curved and disappeared through Kennaway Tunnel, a gaping hole bored into the red sandstone cliff. 'It's just around the corner from the boathouse. It will be quieter there.'

'I've looked on the map, and there's another cove along the coast towards Teignmouth.' Percy indicated further up the shore. 'They have better rocks there.'

'We'd have to climb that hill,' I complained. The idea was unappealing in the July heat.

'The rocks here are fine for what I need,' Millicent said, to my relief.

'But this is a smugglers' cove. My car's just over there. I'll drive us.'

This decided it, and we crossed the bridge over the railway line to where Percy's Ford Roadster was parked on Marine Parade.

'Is this where you're staying?' I asked. The red cliffs rose up directly behind a row of boarding houses and hotels. At the end of the parade was the Blenheim Hotel, where the wedding reception would be held.

'At the Jewel of the Sea.' He gestured to a large house painted pale pink with its name ornately written in sea green above the door. A middle-aged lady with unlikely red curls and crimson lips stood by a bay window. She waved enthusiastically at Percy, and he waved back.

'Who's that?' I asked.

'My landlady. Miss Emerald Dubois. A fascinating lady.'

'How exotic,' Millicent observed.

'I don't think it's her real name,' Percy said seriously.

'You don't say,' I remarked.

'She used to be on the stage. Had to give it up because of her ankles. She has lots of theatrical friends. Some of them board with her when they're in town. She has two staying with her at the moment. They're appearing in *The Second Mrs Tanqueray* at the Theatre Royal in Exeter. We should go and see it.'

'How appropriate,' I murmured. 'A play about a second wife with a dubious past.'

'Katherine does not have a dubious past,' Millicent protested.

Percy was more interested in smugglers than second wives. 'Emerald's been telling me about the smuggling that used to go on along this stretch of coastline. In the fourteenth century, a smuggler from around these parts called Dick Endicott was shot dead by an exciseman. Endicott's ghost is said to roam Smugglers

Cove in search of the treasure he hid in the caves there. Gold and jewellery.'

'We're going on a treasure hunt?' I asked, amused. 'Don't you think any gold might have been found by now?'

'No harm in sniffing around for old Dick's ill-gotten gains, is there?'

We got into the car and Percy drove to the end of Marine Parade, took a sharp left up to Teignmouth Hill, climbing up to Teignmouth Road. When the road curved towards the cliff edge, Percy pulled over into a lay-by. A wooden fingerpost sign was engraved with the words 'Smugglers Cove' and pointed to a path leading down the cliff.

Millicent peered at the sign. 'Was there more than one smuggler?'

'Hundreds, I should think,' Percy replied. 'Why?'

'I'm wondering where to put the missing apostrophe on that sign,' Millicent said pensively. 'After the r or the s.'

'Good grief, woman. Leave the sign alone. They've dispensed with apostrophes in these parts.'

We got out of the car and cautiously went to the cliff's edge to take in the view. Yellow evening primrose covered the ochre-red sandstone rocks that overlooked the glistening sea below. I'd been quite content to wander along the beach at Dawlish but had to admit the view from the cliff was enticing.

'Are you game?' Percy was clearly desperate to explore the cove.

Millicent was less enthusiastic. 'It's a steep path.'

'But it will be worth the trek,' he promised.

The beach below was inviting – a perfectly enclosed cove with smooth golden sand. And even better, it was deserted. However, to get to it, we had to clamber down a rough footpath, which led to a foot crossing over the railway line.

From Dawlish, the railway line passed through two tunnels before it reached this point. To our left, we could see the track emerge from Coryton Tunnel, and to our right, it disappeared again into Phillot Tunnel. After this, it would travel through Clerk's Tunnel, emerge onto a section of sea wall at Breeches Rock, before disappearing again into Parsons Tunnel and going on to Teignmouth.

'Come on then.' Millicent hitched up her long skirt and led the way. Although my shoes weren't as stout as hers, they were robust enough to tackle the cliff path. We began to scramble down, and I saw that to our left was a picturesque villa with white walls that gleamed in the sunshine. It was set back from where the tunnel ran through the rock and had a tiered garden filled with Mediterranean-looking trees and flowers. The last tier of the garden sat directly over the tunnel, and from it led a winding slope down to the cove.

'Imagine living there.' I wondered what it must be like to wake to such a glorious view each morning.

The path became easier the lower we got. Finally, we reached the crossing and once over the railway line, it was a short distance to the beach below. The tide was going out and the sand was smooth and firm to walk on.

'We have the whole beach to ourselves.' Percy started to take off his shoes. 'Let's paddle.'

'I thought you wanted to look for treasure?' I said.

'I need to cool off first.'

'I'm going to explore the caves and take some rock samples.' Millicent reached into her bag and fished out her hammer and chisel.

The sea was too tempting. I pulled off my shoes and peeled down my stockings to join Percy. The feeling of cold water running over my feet was delicious. I breathed in the clean, salty air and let my worries dissolve. I was in this beautiful place with two close friends, and for the moment, life felt good.

'Wasn't this a brilliant idea of mine?' Percy was highly pleased with himself. He'd been the one to persuade me to come down before the wedding and have a holiday.

'For once, I think you were right.'

Strolling along the shore reminded me of the time I'd spent in the south of France, although the heat and smells were very different there. I imagined being back with George, walking hand in hand along the beach in Nice.

'What are you thinking about?' Percy asked.

'Nothing in particular.'

Percy didn't react well to any mention of my scandalous trip abroad. He'd been hostile on my return, and I didn't want to raise the spectre of George. Not when we were getting on so well. I turned my thoughts away from the south of France back to this distinctly British coastline, letting a feeling of calm wash over me.

The peace was short-lived. Hearing a series of thuds, we turned to see Millicent had fallen backwards. A gull and a crow, fighting over a string of seaweed, flew up in alarm.

'What happened?' Percy called.

Millicent was sitting on the beach with a dazed expression on her face. She didn't reply, so we waded out of the water and went over.

'Are you hurt?' I dropped onto the sand beside her. I noticed she'd dislodged some pretty big boulders from the cliff face.

She shook her head. 'I managed to jump out of the way. There's a cave, and...' She blinked. 'There's something in it. I think it's a person.'

Percy scrambled over the boulders and peered into the cavern. 'Bloody hell.'

I jumped up and, struggling in my bare feet, navigated around the rocks to peer over his shoulder.

'Oh.' I gripped Percy's arm.

A skeletal hand peeked out from the sleeve of a brown tweed jacket.

3

Percy and I edged our way into the cave exposed by the rock fall. It was around twelve feet deep by twelve feet high. The entrance appeared to have been strengthened by some old stone walling. It smelt ancient and musty.

The man was in a seated position, propped against the back wall. His skeletal body was hidden by the fabric of a suit and overcoat, but the skull was exposed.

Millicent came up behind us but backed away as soon as she got too close. 'I can't look.'

She began to examine the walls of the cavern instead. They were smooth and the vaulted roof had clearly been enlarged by hand. Millicent inspected the grey stones that contrasted with the rich red of the sandstone rocks.

'This has been here for centuries. It probably started out as a fisherman's cellar. A place to keep nets, ropes, barrels, salt, and fish. It could be up to five hundred years old.'

'Do you think that's the remains of a fisherman?' Percy whispered, as though the skeleton could hear him.

'Wearing a suit and overcoat?' I replied. 'He's dressed warmly.

That's a thick tweed suit and heavy woollen overcoat. And he's got sturdy leather boots on.'

'He must have been here since winter. Perhaps he was exploring the caves and there was a storm and he got trapped by a rock fall.' Millicent shuddered.

'Not the winter just gone.' I regarded the skeletal remains. 'He's been here longer than that.'

Percy pulled at my arm. 'Be careful in case any more rocks come down. I don't fancy ending up like our friend here.'

We edged out of the cave, and Millicent retrieved her hammer and chisel from where she'd thrown them, tucking them back in her bag.

'I was looking at these smaller caves.' She ran her hand along the cliff where there were a series of shallow alcoves. 'I saw these rocks were a little different, and when I tapped with my hammer, one of the boulders toppled, and the others became dislodged.'

'I wonder how long the body's been in there,' I said. 'We'll have to tell the police.'

'Hey there.'

We jumped at the sound of someone shouting and turned to see a tall, well-built gentleman of about fifty striding across the beach. He must have come from the villa on the cliff.

'This is a private beach.' Close up, I could see he had brown hair, greying at the temples, tense blue eyes and an expression that was far from welcoming. 'You're trespassing.'

'We're here on holiday. We came down that public footpath.' Percy motioned towards the railway crossing.

'Is that your house?' I asked. 'Do you have a telephone?'

'No. Why?' He seemed taken aback by the question.

'I'm afraid we've uncovered what seems to be a body,' Millicent explained.

'A what?'

'A skeleton. Human remains,' Percy added helpfully.

'Washed up on the beach?' he asked, but his eyes went to the cliff and he took in the fallen rocks.

Millicent gestured towards the cave. 'Perhaps. Or they may have been killed by a rock fall.'

The man navigated the boulders to peer inside the cave. He quickly withdrew. 'I suppose you're right. It could have been a rock fall.'

I was glad Millicent had returned the hammer and chisel to the depths of her bag.

'We need to inform the police,' I said.

He stared at the entrance to the cave. We watched in silence, waiting for him to respond.

Eventually, Percy cleared his throat. 'Would you like us to inform the police? You say this is your beach?'

The man seemed to come to his senses. 'Sorry. It's the shock. I'll drive into town and fetch Sergeant Norsworthy. I'm Captain Rupert Keats. I live at Smugglers Haunt.' He nodded towards the cliff house. 'You'd better stay here until we return.'

We watched as he made his way across the beach to the slope that led up to the villa.

'Keats,' Millicent said. 'Do you think he's related to Katherine?'

'I'm not sure. I suppose it's likely.' I was more interested in the skeleton than Katherine's relatives and moved closer to get a better look. 'Could it have been washed up?'

Millicent didn't seem to want to get too near to the body. She stepped back to examine the cliff. 'It's possible, although the sea would have had to have washed it into the cave before the rock fall. I think it's more likely he was killed by the rocks falling.'

'But there are no signs of injury. The skull looks intact.' I leant in to inspect the skeleton.

'Ugh. You're not going to touch it?' She screwed up her face in disgust.

'He's sitting up, leaning against the back of the cave. It's like he stopped to take a rest and got trapped.'

'Come out of there, Iris,' Percy protested. 'It's not nice to poke around in some poor blighter's bones.'

'He still has some hair. It's dark. Almost black,' I observed. 'And there's a ring on his wedding finger. It's unusual. Silver engraved with tiny doves.'

'You're unnaturally ghoulish. Don't touch his hand. It might fall off.'

Millicent winced.

Percy scrambled over the boulders and walked towards the sea.

'Where are you going?' I called.

'To put my shoes and socks on,' he said over his shoulder. 'I'm not meeting members of the Devonshire constabulary in my bare feet.'

I'd forgotten I wasn't wearing any shoes or stockings. I left the body and went after Percy.

We sat on the beach and waited until we saw Rupert coming down the slope of Smugglers Haunt with a policeman in tow.

'Unless he asks you directly, it might be best not to mention you bashed the rocks with your hammer and chisel,' Percy remarked. 'That Keats chap could get nasty about you damaging his property.'

Millicent nodded. We rose as they approached.

'This is Sergeant Norsworthy of Dawlish Police.'

The sergeant removed his hat to reveal a bald crown circled by dark grey hair. His thick moustache was of a similar shade of grey. Millicent indicated the cavern, and he stepped forward to peer inside.

'How on earth did he get there?'

No one had an answer to this. Sergeant Norsworthy spent a few moments scrutinising the cave, then turned to Percy. 'You found him?'

'My friend Miss Nightingale found him.' Percy nodded towards Millicent. 'Miss Woodmore and I were in the sea when we heard her call out.'

'I wanted to take a few rock samples to show my pupils. I'm a schoolteacher. I must have tapped in the wrong spot as it led to this.' Millicent made it sound as though she'd tapped the cliff with her hand. She gestured to the boulders lying around us.

Sergeant Norsworthy inspected Millicent and then the rocks. He seemed to decide that she was telling the truth. He stroked his moustache, which I noticed Percy was examining with interest. Waving his hand in the direction of the body, he said, 'Don't need a doctor to tell us he's dead.'

Again, there was no answer to this.

'Woodmore.' Captain Keats regarded me. 'Are you related to the chap Katherine's marrying?'

'Thomas Woodmore is my father,' I replied.

'Katherine was married to my brother, Laurence.' His face lost its former scowl and he smiled graciously. 'Sorry if I was a bit abrupt earlier. It's just that we get a lot of trespassers in the summer. You and your friends are welcome to visit the cove any time while you're here.'

The mysterious Major Laurence Keats. I hadn't particularly warmed to Rupert, and it appeared I was about to become associated with his family. I was attempting to find something civil to say when Percy saved me the bother by commenting inanely that Mrs Keats obviously had excellent taste in men.

Rupert Keats' eyebrows shot up in surprise, then he gave a

short laugh. 'You must be right. I'm delighted for Katherine. She's invited my wife and me to the wedding.'

Was there anyone Katherine hadn't invited to this damn wedding? The church was going to be packed to the rafters.

Sergeant Norsworthy coughed. 'I'll need to take your names and addresses. Perhaps, Captain Keats, we could do this up at the house rather than down here?' He indicated towards the body.

'Of course. I'm sure you're in need of some refreshment. It must have been a terrible shock to come across this, er, poor gentleman.' Rupert Keats' hostility of earlier had been replaced by ingratiating politeness and a forced affability.

'That's decent of you. I'm parched.' Percy strode after Rupert.

Millicent seemed reluctant to leave her find. She turned to Sergeant Norsworthy. 'What will happen to him?'

'When Captain Keats told me what you'd discovered, I telephoned the pathologist at the Royal Devon & Exeter Hospital. He's bringing a couple of his students with him to take a look at this chap. My constables have gone to fetch a stretcher and they'll help to get the bones out of the cave and up to the ambulance.'

'Where will they take him?' she asked.

'To the morgue at the hospital, where he'll be examined.'

Sergeant Norsworthy started to trudge along the beach, and after a last glance at the cave, we followed.

The slope up to Smugglers Haunt was a much easier incline than the steep path we'd taken down to the cove. It wound its way up to a three-tiered garden that was an unusual mix of weather-beaten palm trees and hardy perennials.

Rupert Keats showed us through a side door of the villa into a spacious living room with a panoramic window that looked out over the coastline. A young woman had been watching our progress up the slope and through the garden, and she came forward to greet us.

To my surprise, Captain Keats introduced her as his wife, Nathalie. I would have assumed she was his daughter.

Nathalie Keats was extraordinary to look at, with rosebud lips, pale blonde hair and delicate porcelain features. There was something familiar about her, though I knew I would have remembered if I'd met her before.

'I've asked Mrs Green to make some tea. It must have been a dreadful shock for you.' Nathalie spoke perfect English with a slight accent I couldn't place. 'Please sit down.'

'What a view.' Percy, who'd gone straight over to the window, came to join us on the sofa. He seemed as entranced by Nathalie as he was by the scenery.

'Not bad, is it? Smugglers Cove comes with the villa. It belonged to my father.' Rupert gazed at Nathalie as he said this and I got the impression he took as much pride in his wife as he did his home.

The door opened and a woman entered carrying a tray. She appeared to be about seventy, although her hair was jet black. It reminded me of the tufts of hair on the skeleton in the cave, except that Mrs Green's hair was obviously dyed and didn't move, sitting on her head like a helmet.

'Thank you, Mrs Green. We can manage.' Captain Keats took the tray from her. From the woman's look of surprise, Rupert didn't usually take charge of the tea pouring. Reluctantly, she handed him the tray, and after considering everyone in the room, she left. I strongly suspected she hadn't gone far and was hovering outside the door, listening.

Rupert began to fuss with the tea things. 'I'm sure you're in need of a strong cup of tea after the shock you've had, Miss Nightingale.'

Millicent gratefully took the cup he offered.

'Did you know the cave was there?' I asked.

Nathalie shook her head, but Rupert nodded.

'My brother and I used to play in it as children. There are caves like it all along the coast. Old fisherman's cellars. I'm not sure when it got filled in.'

We drank the tea, and Sergeant Norsworthy wrote down the addresses of where we were staying. 'It's just for our records. I'm sure they'll be no need for me to bother you with any more questions.'

'I'd like to hear what you find out about this man,' Millicent said.

Sergeant Norsworthy gave her a grim smile. 'I'm not sure there will be much to tell. The coroner will hold an inquest and probably decide this poor fella, whoever he is, died in an unfortunate accident.'

'But you'll carry out an investigation?'

The sergeant sighed. 'I'll certainly ask around to see if anyone knows anything.'

Mrs Green reappeared at the door. 'Your constables are here, Sergeant Norsworthy. And the men from the hospital.'

'Thank you, Mrs Green.' Captain Keats stood up. 'I'll show our guests out and then take them down to the cove.'

We hastily finished our tea and rose to leave. I'd have liked to have watched them remove the skeleton from the cave, but it was clear we were being dismissed. Rupert showed us out to the driveway at the front of the house.

'Fortunately, it's downhill back to Dawlish,' he said cheerily.

'Daddy!' A small boy of about four appeared and peeked at us from behind his father's legs. He had his mother's striking features and I was struck again by a sense of familiarity.

'Back inside, Timothy,' Rupert ordered and shut the door.

Dawlish may have been downhill, but Percy's car was parked further up from the villa. We followed the winding driveway back to the road, then trudged up the hill to the lay-by.

Before we got in the car, we looked over the cliff to Smugglers Haunt. Captain Keats was leading a group of men down the slope to the beach. Sergeant Norsworthy was talking to a gentleman carrying a black medical bag. They were followed by two police constables carrying a stretcher between them, and two young men we presumed were the doctor's medical students. Above them, Nathalie Keats watched from the window.

Percy's eyes were fixed on her. 'How on earth did that heavenly young creature end up married to an old grump like him?'

'I'm more curious to know why there's a body hidden on their private beach,' I commented. 'Rupert Keats showed a remarkable lack of concern for this man. Wouldn't you think he'd be more curious about a body being found in a cave he used to play in as a child?'

'And I don't think Sergeant Norsworthy intends to make much of an effort to find out who the man is,' Millicent added. 'I intend to call on him next week to enquire about the progress he's made.'

Percy and I exchanged an amused glance. Millicent clearly wasn't going to trust the sergeant with her discovery.

4

'I'm not sure Dawlish police station will welcome a visit from us,' Percy said. 'It's not a usual tourist destination.'

We'd spent the weekend sightseeing on Dartmoor, walking through Widecombe-in-the-Moor, climbing Haytor Rock and exploring its old quarry and the remains of a granite tramway that had been constructed a century before. Nine miles of granite tracks had linked five quarries before descending thirteen hundred feet to the Stover Canal.

As fascinated as Millicent had been by the granite structure, I knew she was itching to find out more about our mystery man. After you discover a skeleton on the first day of your holiday, nothing else seems quite as exciting.

When Percy had dropped us off at my grandparents on Sunday evening, she'd asked him to find out where Dawlish police station was.

On Monday morning, we found Percy seated on a bench by the brook that ran through the centre of the town. A pair of black swans pecked the grass at his feet. He'd become extremely attached to the birds and was feeding them a slice of toast he'd sneaked from the boarding house at breakfast.

'Friendly creatures,' he observed.

'Why are there black swans here?' Millicent asked.

'About twenty years ago, some chap from New Zealand gave them to the town as a gift. He was born in Dawlish and came back on frequent visits. He thought a few black swans would liven the place up a bit.' Percy fed the last of the toast to the birds and stood up. 'Come on then, let's go and find Sergeant Norsworthy.'

'Perhaps it would be best if we didn't all go into the police station,' I commented, though I didn't want to be left behind.

'I'm going in,' Millicent retorted. 'He's my skeleton.'

Percy turned to her. 'You've become very possessive over this pile of bones.'

'I found him and I want to know who he is. You can stay here with your swans if you want.'

'I'm not missing out on all the fun.'

We walked across the green to The Strand, and the swans followed. They took no notice when Percy knelt down to explain to them that we'd be even less welcome at the police station if they accompanied us. We were saved by the arrival of a family who spread out a blanket on the grass and placed a picnic basket on it. The swans waddled over expectantly.

'The police station is up here.' Percy directed us away from the shops on The Strand, up Queen Street and left onto Park Road. We spotted a blue police lamp fixed to the wall of an unassuming building.

Inside, we were greeted by a young constable standing behind a battered wooden front desk. His welcoming smile faded when we asked to see Sergeant Norsworthy. He obviously knew the effect this request was likely to have on his senior officer. 'Could I ask what it's concerning?'

Millicent explained that she'd been the one to discover the body at Smugglers Cove as if this conveyed some rights upon her.

He nodded gloomily. 'Wait here.'

The row of wooden chairs lined up against the wall were as uncomfortable as they looked. Millicent wrinkled her nose at the pungent odour of disinfectant.

'I don't suppose they want to make the place too cosy.' Percy stretched out his long legs. 'I wonder what the cells are like?'

'I'm hoping we won't find out,' I replied.

The young constable reappeared, looking more cheerful. 'This way.'

The police station was tiny, and we followed single file down a narrow corridor. I hoped more than one person didn't commit a crime in the town at any given time. Two criminals would be a tight squeeze.

To our surprise, Sergeant Norsworthy didn't seem too put out to see us.

'Sit down,' he ordered.

We sat.

'I have some news for you.' The sergeant looked pleased with himself. 'I believe the body you found is that of Mr Arnold Rowe.'

'Gosh.' Percy scratched his head. 'Who is, or was, Arnold Rowe?'

'A smuggler.'

'A smuggler?' Percy gave a sideways glance towards Millicent and me. He clearly thought Sergeant Norsworthy was not all there. 'The body didn't appear that old.'

The policeman gave him a withering look. 'I'm not suggesting he was some sort of pirate. Smuggling still goes on along the coast, especially now we've got fewer coastguard stations to keep an eye out for ships in distress.'

'Does it?' Percy was delighted. 'What do smugglers smuggle nowadays, if you don't mind me asking?'

'Spirits and tobacco mainly. Trying to avoid paying taxes.'

'Oh, I see.' Percy was undoubtedly hoping for something a little more glamorous, but he was still interested. 'And this chap, Arnold Rowe, went in for that sort of thing?'

'Been at it for years. Used to go out in a small boat to meet larger vessels bringing contraband in from the continent. He's known locally for trading in all sorts of goods.'

'When did Mr Rowe go missing?' Millicent asked.

'His wife reported his disappearance in December 1918. She hadn't seen him for a couple of weeks. She expected him to show his face at Christmas or at least contact her. Mr Rowe used to do odd jobs up at Smugglers Haunt. The skeleton is male and about the right height.'

Millicent's eyes widened. 'He's been in the cave for nearly five years?'

'Since the tenth of December 1918.'

'That's astonishing,' Percy exclaimed. 'You can tell that from modern science?'

'There was a train ticket in the pocket of Mr Rowe's suit,' Sergeant Norsworthy replied dryly.

'A train ticket?' I asked. 'Where from?'

'Third class return ticket from Teignmouth to Dawlish.'

'Did Arnold Rowe live in Teignmouth?'

'No. He lived in Dawlish.'

'Then why would he return to Teignmouth?'

'I'm not in a position to ask him, am I?' Sergeant Norsworthy snapped, evidently irritated by my interrogation.

'Did you find anything else in the man's pockets?' I couldn't stop myself from asking more questions.

'No.'

'What about a wallet?'

'No.'

'Isn't that odd?' Despite Percy poking me in the ribs, I kept quizzing the sergeant.

The policeman sighed. 'He might have left it up at the house. Or dropped it.'

'In the cave?'

'Nothing was found in the cave. He could have dropped it on the beach and it got washed away,' Sergeant Norsworthy growled in exasperation.

Millicent decided to intervene at this point. 'How did Mr Rowe die?'

'Natural causes.'

'Natural causes?' Percy repeated in disbelief.

The sergeant backtracked. 'The cause of death will be for the coroner to decide at the inquest. There were no marks on the bones to indicate he was subjected to any injury. His body must have just given out.'

'How old was Mr Rowe?' Millicent asked.

'He was thirty years old when he went missing.'

'Was he in good health?'

'He was deemed no longer physically fit for war service and discharged from the army in the June of that year. He had problems with his feet. Not bad enough to stop him from falling into his old ways as soon as he got home though.'

'So how exactly did he end up in a cave at the foot of a cliff?' I said, more to myself than in the expectation of an answer.

Sergeant Norsworthy shrugged. 'Tragic accident. Probably up to no good. These things happen.'

I thought it highly unlikely that these things did just happen. Did smugglers wear suits and overcoats nowadays? And travel by train rather than boat?

'But he was found on a private beach,' I said. 'If he were meeting a boat, surely it would have been seen from the house?'

'Not if it was dark,' he replied. 'Smugglers avoid anywhere close to the coastguard's lookout, which is on the cliff along from the railway station. Boats come from the west into the coves between Dawlish and Teignmouth or to the east of the town. The caves under Langstone Rock were traditionally used. But that was back when smuggling was big business and the smugglers hid out on Dawlish Warren.'

'Wouldn't Mr Rowe have chosen a cove that was accessible by road? To get to the road from Smugglers Cove, he'd have had to climb the cliff via a steep footpath that would be treacherous at night,' I mused. 'Or go through the garden of Smugglers Haunt.'

'Perhaps that's what he did. As I said, he used to do odd jobs at the villa.' Sergeant Norsworthy stood up. 'I'll show you out.'

The young constable at the desk gave us a cheery smile as we were firmly ushered through the door onto the street.

We wandered back to the bench by the brook, and Percy attempted to lure the black swans over to him by making strange cooing noises.

'Poor Arnold Rowe,' Millicent murmured.

I frowned. 'A smuggler who wears a suit and travels by train.'

'You don't think it's him?' Millicent said.

'I suppose it must be if he went missing at that time and worked at Smugglers Haunt. What I don't understand is how he ended up dead in that cave. It doesn't make sense.'

'I don't think it's something Sergeant Norsworthy intends to investigate,' Millicent commented. 'He's no Ben Gilbert.'

She was referring to my childhood friend who'd been the local constable in Walden and was presently working for the Metropolitan police.

I nodded. 'Ben's thorough and keeps an open mind until he has factual evidence. Norsworthy strikes me as lazy.'

'Mr Rowe deserves justice. We should speak to Sergeant Norsworthy's superior officer.' It seemed Millicent wasn't prepared to let this go.

Percy stroked his annoying moustache. 'I don't think we'll hold much sway with the Devonshire Constabulary.'

'We need someone to exert some influence,' she replied.

Like Millicent, I wanted to find out more about this man. I didn't feel her sense of protectiveness over the skeleton, but I was curious to know what had befallen Arnold Rowe. Even if he was a villain, it wasn't right that he'd been hidden in a cave for five years.

'Do you know anyone of influence?' Millicent asked.

'I know a local solicitor. Stephen Damerell is Katherine's brother. He and my father went to Ladysmith Boys' School together. It's where my grandfather taught. I haven't seen Stephen and his wife Gwendolen since I was a child. I should call on them to say I'm here.'

'If this Arnold Rowe is a local villain, their paths may have crossed,' Percy commented.

I nodded. 'And there's always Horace.'

Millicent looked at me in surprise. 'Does his influence extend this far?'

I smiled. 'Horace has contacts everywhere.'

* * *

'You've found something to investigate already?' Horace Laffaye raised a finger, and a waiter was immediately by his side. 'How exciting. Just what we need to liven up our sojourn here.'

Percy had left his car outside the boarding house and taken

the train with Millicent and me to Exeter St David's Station. We'd strolled to the Rougemont Hotel on Queen Street, and he'd whistled at the ornate exterior. 'I say. This is rather splendid.'

The inside was as lavish as the outside. The entrance hall was a magnificent, vast space with high-panelled ceilings supported by Doric columns. Enormous displays of flowers appeared at intervals along the sides of the hall, filling the air with the scent of roses and lilies.

We'd found Horace and Elijah seated in the lounge on plush red leather armchairs. Percy was delighted to join the two men in a whisky and soda and even more delighted by the cigar Horace offered him. Millicent and I opted for a sherry, a tipple I'd begun to enjoy since being introduced to it by Millicent and her Great Aunt Ursula.

'Tell all,' Horace instructed.

I told the tale of poor Arnold Rowe, with frequent interruptions from Millicent and Percy. Elijah puffed on his cigar, regarding us with amusement.

'I agree. I think a little more investigation into this man's death is required.' Horace swirled the ice cubes around his glass. 'I'll telephone Miss Vale and ask her to make some calls. See if we can arrange to have a chat with the senior officer for this region.'

Percy grinned, no doubt picturing the look on Sergeant Norsworthy's face when he received a call from his boss.

Elijah wasn't as happy. 'You say this Captain Keats is Laurence's brother?'

I nodded. 'He and his wife, Nathalie, are coming to the wedding. He seemed a pleasant man. Keen to help the police.'

I noticed Millicent and Percy exchange a dubious glance at my last comment. Rupert Keats hadn't been thrilled to involve the police and had shown a strange lack of curiosity about the body.

But Elijah wouldn't be willing to help if he thought I'd taken against someone from Katherine's family.

To my relief, he seemed to accept this and made no further comment. I sipped my sherry. Would it upset the wedding plans if Captain Keats was found to have been involved in this man's death? Too bad if it did. If Arnold Rowe was murdered, he deserved justice.

5

'What's the plan for this morning, ladies?' Percy greeted us as we emerged from Dawlish railway station.

'We thought we'd pay a visit to Smugglers Cove. Captain Keats said we were welcome to visit the beach while we were here,' I replied.

'Good idea. Especially as the captain won't be there.'

'How do you know?' I suspected Percy was keen to see the lovely Nathalie again.

'I saw him earlier. He was off to his shop.'

'What shop?'

'Emerald was telling me he's retired from the army now. He's a wine importer and has a premises in Exeter.'

Percy drove up the hill and parked in the lay-by. We wanted to nose around the cave again before we called at the house, which meant navigating our way down the steep path and over the railway crossing. The beach was glorious in the sunshine, and the sea a flat shimmering surface. I wished I'd bought my swimsuit.

Percy had the same thought. 'Let's ask Mrs Keats if she'd mind us bringing a picnic here one day. We could take a bathe.'

Millicent was more interested in getting back to the cave. It was as we'd left it, minus the skeleton and not as smelly as it had been before. Without a skull staring up at her, Millicent was happier to explore every crevice.

After examining the cave and then the boulders lying on the ground at the entrance, she announced, 'Someone put him there deliberately.'

I agreed. 'I think he was hidden on purpose.'

'You can't be certain,' Percy objected.

'The body was propped up against the wall. Sergeant Norsworthy said there were no broken bones.'

'He could have been concussed without fracturing his skull.'

'In which case, I'd have expected him to be lying down,' I said.

'There was something odd about the way the rocks were positioned.' Millicent gestured to the boulders strewn around the entrance to the cave. 'I can't explain it, but it didn't look like a natural formation. I think they were stacked that way.'

'That's not something we could prove now.' I inspected the stones scattered over the sand.

'I could be wrong, it's just the impression I got.' Millicent looked towards the railway line. 'Is that Parsons Tunnel?'

'No, that's further along towards Teignmouth. Why?'

'The author Maurice Drake lives in this area. In his book, *The Ocean Sleuth*, mysterious events take place in Parsons Tunnel. I wondered if something could have happened to this man on the railway track or in the tunnel.' Millicent and her great aunt were keen readers of crime novels.

'I don't think our man has been anywhere near the railway line except in the carriage of a train,' Percy remarked.

'More likely, he was put there. And I don't think someone carried him down the cliff path and over the rail track. Much easier to get him here from the house.' I looked over to Smugglers Haunt. The sloped curving path made the descent much gentler.

Millicent narrowed her eyes and squinted up at the villa. 'That would mean someone at Smugglers Haunt must be involved.'

'Not Nathalie,' Percy said firmly. 'Too delicate.'

This was true. If it had been Nathalie, she'd have had to have killed the man where he lay. I didn't say this to Percy. 'That leaves Captain Keats.'

'Here's the man himself,' Millicent said. 'And there's someone with him.'

Two men were strolling down the slope from the garden of Smugglers Haunt.

'I don't think that's Rupert Keats...' I began, then stopped.

'What is it?' Millicent asked.

I couldn't believe what I was seeing. Or, to be more precise, who I was seeing. As the two men got closer, there could be no doubt.

'Iris. It is you.' A tall blond man ran across the sand and swept me up in an enthusiastic embrace.

'Emile,' I gasped. 'Marc.'

The second man was less exuberant but said with a smile, 'It's good to see you again, Iris.'

The last time I'd seen Emile Vandamme and Marc Jansen was in June 1917 at the Park Fever Hospital in Hither Green when it had been given over to housing Belgian refugees. I'd been posted there after I'd joined the Voluntary Aid Detachment.

I introduced Marc and Emile to Percy and Millicent. 'What are you doing here in Devon?' I asked. 'I thought you would have returned to Belgium.'

'Nathalie and I decided to stay,' Emile replied. 'Nathalie's my sister.'

'The one you were searching for?'

That's why Nathalie Keats had seemed so familiar. She had the same high cheekbones and facial features as Emile. They also shared the same fair hair and blue eyes. Nathalie's son, Timothy, looked like a younger version of his uncle.

Marc and Emile had arrived at the Park Fever Hospital anxious for news of their families, who they believed had been housed in Devon. Emile's sister and parents had fled Belgium after Germany had invaded in 1914 and travelled to England with Marc's wife and parents. Emile and Marc had stayed in Belgium to fight in the resistance but had been forced to flee in 1917.

At that time, my grandmother had been working as a volunteer in the refugee centre in Exeter. I'd written to her and she'd been able to locate their families.

Emile nodded. 'When Nathalie said someone called Iris Woodmore had discovered a body in the cliffs, we thought it must be our Iris.'

'It was actually Millicent who found him.'

'What a dreadful thing to have happened.' Emile turned his attention to her. 'I hope it hasn't ruined your holiday.'

'Not at all.' Millicent flushed, gazing into his concerned blue eyes.

I remembered seeing the same rapt expression on the faces of the volunteers at the hospital. Women would glance at Emile from under their lashes while Marc watched in amusement at the effect his friend was having. Not that Marc was unattractive, with his soulful brown eyes and warm smile. But next to Emile, who could set pulses racing, he happily faded into the background.

Marc and I exchanged a brief smile.

'How is your wife?' I racked my brain for a name and was pleased when it came to me. 'Annette.'

'She's well, thank you. She's up at the house with Nathalie.'

Marc gestured to Smugglers Haunt. 'My parents returned to Belgium after the war, but we decided to stay. We live in Exeter, and I work for Stephen Damerell's law firm. I have your grandparents to thank for that. How are Bartholomew and Clementina?'

'They're very well.' I turned to Emile. 'What are you doing now?'

'I'm a chef at the Royal Clarence Hotel in Exeter.'

'How exciting,' Millicent exclaimed. 'Do you cook for famous people?'

'Sometimes,' Emile said with a smile. 'I hope I'll have the opportunity to cook for you while you're here.'

I doubted it, as the Royal Clarence was out of our price range.

'My parents also returned to Belgium,' Emile continued. 'But I wanted to stay. And by that time, Nathalie was engaged to Captain Keats.'

Was it my imagination, or was there a flicker of disdain on Emile's face when he mentioned his brother-in-law? Rupert Keats was undoubtedly a lot older than his wife.

'Nathalie tells us you're here for your father's wedding,' Marc said.

I nodded. 'I came down early with my friends for a holiday. Millicent and I are staying with my grandparents in Exeter.'

'What about you, Mr Baverstock? Where are you staying?' Marc asked politely.

'Call me Percy. I'm at the Jewel of the Sea in Dawlish.'

'Emerald's place.' Emile smirked. It seemed Miss Dubois had quite a reputation.

'That's right. Charming lady. Speaking of charming ladies, we were just about to call on your sister,' Percy added hopefully.

'Percee is right.' Emile stretched out the cee sound. 'Let us go and find Nathalie.'

'Percy,' Percy corrected in a clipped tone.

'Percee.' Emile nodded, looking momentarily confused. Then he set off towards the house, clasping Millicent's hand and helping her over some washed-up seaweed.

Marc asked if I still lived near the hospital in Hither Green. I told him my father and I had moved from London to my childhood home of Walden, and that I worked as a journalist for the local paper. I glanced back at Percy, who seemed a little disconcerted by these new male attractions. But as we neared the house, he brightened at the sight of Nathalie Keats coming down the slope to greet us, accompanied by a shorter, dark-haired woman who I presumed must be Annette Jansen.

'It is our Iris,' Emile announced. 'From the hospital in London.'

To my surprise, Nathalie came forward to embrace me. 'I should have realised who you were last week. I'm so grateful to you and your darling grandmother for helping Emile and Marc to find us. Annette and I had begun to fear we'd lost them.' Her pale blue eyes filled with tears, and the effect was mesmerising.

Percy was gazing at her, a soppy expression on his face.

Annette took Nathalie's place and gave me a shy hug.

Embarrassed by this affection, I muttered, 'I'm so glad your families were reunited.'

Nathalie took my arm. 'I've asked Mrs Green to bring drinks out to the terrace.'

She led us up the slope to a patio furnished with bistro style tables and cushioned iron chairs.

'Uncle Emile.' Timothy came running out of the house. Emile swept this miniature version of himself up in his arms. 'I've got a new train, Uncle Marc.' The boy waved the toy at him.

Marc took Timothy from Emile. 'Then we must build you a bigger railway station.'

'Do you have children too?' The affection between these families made me feel quite emotional, knowing what they'd endured before being reunited and starting afresh in a foreign country.

Marc shook his head.

Annette smiled. 'But we hope to one day.'

While Nathalie was tall and fair, Annette was a petite, pretty woman with gamine features, large brown eyes and glossy, almost-black hair.

'Nathalie tells me you're here for your father's wedding. Katherine's a dear friend of ours. She helped us when we first came to Dawlish. You must be looking forward to having a new mama,' Annette said.

Percy sputtered with laughter while I struggled to find an appropriate answer.

Mrs Green appeared, seeming more cheerful than she had on our last visit. She placed a jug of iced lemonade and glasses on the table.

Millicent came to my rescue and changed the subject. 'We spoke to Sergeant Norsworthy yesterday about the body we found.'

'Poor soul.' Marc shook his head sadly. 'I wonder what happened to him. His family must be informed. Even though it's sad news, it's better than living with uncertainty.'

Emile nodded. They had first-hand experience of not knowing what had become of their loved ones.

'Sergeant Norsworthy believes it's a local man called Arnold Rowe,' Millicent said.

Mrs Green gasped and spilt the lemonade she was pouring. 'Arnold. My nephew Arnold?'

6

'I'm so sorry, Mrs Green.' Millicent looked distraught. 'I had no idea Arnold Rowe was your nephew.'

Timothy was staring up at the housekeeper with worried blue eyes, upset by her distress.

'Annette, perhaps you could take Timmy to play?' Nathalie smiled at Annette, who immediately jumped up.

'Of course,' she said, taking his hand. 'Come along, Timmy. Let us play bowls on the lawn.' This was obviously a favourite game as the little boy was immediately distracted and trotted away happily.

I noticed a flash of irritation cross Marc's face and wasn't sure if it was because of Nathalie's presumptuous command or his wife's instant compliance.

Mrs Green was shaking her head in disbelief. 'I thought he'd run away from Joyce. That's his wife. They weren't getting along. Are they sure it's him?'

'Sergeant Norsworthy seems to think so,' Millicent replied. 'He told us Mr Rowe went missing in December 1918. Mrs Rowe has been informed. Do his parents live locally? They should be told too.'

Mrs Green shook her head. 'His mother, my sister, died not long after he was born, and his father died of bronchitis in July 1918.'

'Sergeant Norsworthy said Mr Rowe had been discharged from the army in June 1918,' I said.

'That's right. He cared for his father when he was dying. Then he did casual work around town. He helped out here, doing odd jobs in the house and taking care of the garden, while Joyce did the cleaning. They weren't getting along, and I thought Arnold had just had enough and decided to take off.' Her mouth was set into a grim line. 'I can't believe it's him.'

'Is there any reason why he might have gone into the cave?' I asked.

She shook her head. 'I never saw him go down to the beach. Something's not right about this.'

Nathalie touched her arm. 'This has come as a shock. Why don't you go and rest? I can take care of everything in the house.'

Mrs Green straightened up. 'If you don't mind, Mrs Keats, I'd like to go into town and speak to Sergeant Norsworthy. And Joyce. I'm surprised she hasn't had the decency to come here and tell me about this herself.'

'Of course. Take as long as you need.'

Mrs Green nodded and strode into the house. From her expression, Sergeant Norsworthy and Mrs Rowe were going to get a piece of her mind.

'Did you know this Arnold Rowe?' Emile asked Nathalie.

She shook her head and handed around the glasses of lemonade Mrs Green had poured.

'He was known to be a smuggler,' I said. 'Do you think he could have used the beach here?'

'A smuggler? Here?' Nathalie wrinkled her nose. 'According to locals, this beach hasn't been used for smuggling in centuries.'

'Cutting a railway line through the rocks probably put a stop to it,' Marc commented.

'The police seem to think he may have been up to no good.' Percy smiled his thanks at Nathalie as she handed him a glass. 'Perhaps he was waiting for a boat to arrive and got trapped by the tide or a cliff fall.'

Nathalie didn't seem convinced. 'The water rarely rises that high up the beach, though I suppose it might in a winter storm. It makes me sad to think this man was hidden here for so long. So close to us, and we had no idea.'

Marc frowned. 'Smuggling still goes on in these parts. I've defended a few smugglers in court. But this cove isn't practical. There are plenty of places closer to the road along the coast.'

'Didn't this man have any identification on him? A wallet or something?' Emile asked.

I shook my head. 'According to Sergeant Norsworthy, there was nothing in the pockets of the suit he was wearing.'

Marc looked thoughtful. 'Why are they so certain the body is that of Arnold Rowe?'

'We don't feel that Sergeant Norsworthy has investigated the matter as thoroughly as he should,' Millicent replied.

'He seems to be basing his identification purely on the fact that Mr Rowe went missing in December 1918, and this chap had a train ticket in his pocket dated the tenth of December of that year,' Percy explained.

'Where was the train ticket from?' Marc asked.

'A return from Teignmouth,' I replied.

'Yet this man, Rowe, lived in Dawlish with his wife?' Marc scratched his head. 'Doesn't make sense to me.'

It didn't make sense to me, either.

'As Millicent said, we're not sure Sergeant Norsworthy has bothered to do much investigating. Do you think Stephen would have any influence?' I decided not to mention Horace Laffaye and his contacts at this stage.

'I'll talk to him. See what he thinks,' Marc replied. 'I can't see the cove being used for smuggling any more. Not with regular trains full of tourists passing through.'

'What if this man isn't Mrs Green's nephew, Arnold? She will have been upset for nothing.' Emile raised his hand in a gesture of disgust. 'I will go and see this idiot policeman and tell him what I think of him.'

'No, Emile.' Nathalie reached out and lowered his hand in a placatory gesture. 'It's not our business.'

'Don't go aggravating the police when we don't know the facts,' Marc warned. 'I'll speak to Stephen. He can make discreet enquiries.'

Emile made a 'pah' sound but nodded. I remembered how hot-headed he'd been at the hospital, wanting to jump on the next train to Devon without knowing where he was heading. I'd put it down to his desperation to find his family. Evidently, he still had the same impetuous nature.

'Do you remember any visitors to Smugglers Haunt around that time?' I asked Nathalie.

'Rupert and I were not married then. Annette and I boarded with the local doctor and his wife until the following year. I worked as Dr Frampton's receptionist at his medical practice. Emile and Marc had just returned, and we were making plans for the future.' She smiled at the memory. I could imagine the relief she and Annette must have felt when both men had come home safely.

'Did Captain Keats live here on his own then?' I was becoming more suspicious of Rupert Keats by the minute.

'No. Smugglers Haunt belonged to his brother, Major Keats. Rupert inherited it when Laurence died,' Nathalie explained. 'We moved in after we married.'

I had a strange feeling in the pit of my stomach. 'So in December 1918, Major Keats and Katherine were living here?'

Nathalie nodded. 'That's right.'

7

'Tell me about Emile. How did you come to help him find Nathalie?'

I'd been lying in bed dwelling on the strange circumstances of two men dying at Smugglers Cove within weeks of each other. Millicent's thoughts had obviously been elsewhere.

I smiled in the darkness. We were sharing a bedroom as my father would occupy the second guest room when he arrived.

'When the war started, Father decided it would be best for me to come here to live with Nan and Gramps. I wanted to stay in London.'

I hadn't wanted to leave our house on Hither Green Lane though I didn't tell Millicent this. After my mother died, I still felt close to her when I sat in her bedroom surrounded by her possessions.

'The plan was for me to stay in Exeter for the duration of the war. That was when everyone thought it would be over in months. Nan began to volunteer at 24 Southernhay West and I'd go with her. It was the first provincial centre in the country to welcome Belgian refugees.'

'But you met Emile and Marc in London?'

'When I was seventeen, I decided to go back to Hither Green and join the Voluntary Aid Detachment. I was considered too young for nursing duties, but I could do admin and menial tasks. In 1916, I got a post at the Park Fever Hospital, which had been given over to housing refugees. I lived opposite the hospital on Hither Green Lane.'

'I thought you worked at Lewisham Military Hospital?'

'That was later.' I shuddered, glad Millicent couldn't see me in the dark. My time at Park Fever Hospital hadn't been happy, I was still too raw after my mother's death, but it had been fulfilling. I'd been grateful I could do something to help. My next post at the military hospital had been a relentless parade of casualties – day after day of running around clearing up blood and vomit and washing out bedpans. I pushed thoughts of fatally wounded soldiers from my mind.

'Emile told me he was in the resistance. Is that true?' Millicent sounded awestruck.

'Yes. He and Marc stayed in Belgium to fight while their families came here. They had to flee in June 1917 and were given accommodation at the hospital. Marc was searching for his wife and parents, and Emile for Nathalie and his parents. When she'd first arrived in England, Nathalie had managed to get word to him that they were being put on one of the trains transporting refugees to Devon. After that, he and Marc lost contact with Nathalie and Annette. Hundreds of refugees were given homes in Devon, and it wasn't easy to keep track of where everyone had ended up. I wrote to Nan and she found out that Nathalie Vandamme was boarding with a doctor in Dawlish. Emile and Marc were able to travel to Devon to see their families before they enlisted in the Belgian Army.'

Millicent sighed. 'I'm surprised you didn't keep in touch with Emile. He's very nice-looking.'

I smiled. 'I was eighteen and miserable at that time. I don't think he'd have wanted to keep in touch with me. I've often thought about him and Marc. I'm happy they survived.'

It sounded like an inadequate thing to say. But during my time in the hospitals, I'd come into contact with hundreds of men returning from the battlefields or about to join the fighting. I hadn't wanted to keep in touch with any of them. I'd been too scared of facing more heartache.

* * *

'I'm delighted you could join us for afternoon tea, Superintendent Endicott. So much more civilised than chatting in a police station.' While Horace was clearly relishing having a mystery to enliven his holiday, the superintendent didn't seem happy about his invitation to take tea at the Rougemont Hotel – though summons might have been a better word. He refused the offer of food but accepted a cup of coffee.

The dining room of the hotel was as magnificent as the entrance hall. Endless tables were covered in the whitest of cloths and the shiniest of silver cutlery.

Percy and I had no hesitation in tucking into the tiny sandwiches with their crusts cut off. Millicent delicately ate a sliver of madeira cake.

'Endicott? Any relation to Dick Endicott, the smuggler? The one who's supposed to haunt Smugglers Cove,' Percy asked before popping another salmon and cucumber square into his mouth.

'Not that I'm aware. Endicott is a common Devonshire name,' the superintendent replied without a smile.

'Probably just as well as you'd be on different sides of the law.' Percy seemed oblivious to Superintendent Endicott's hostile glare. 'Mind you, if the missing treasure turned up, I bet you'd be glad to discover he was your however many times great grandfather.'

'Perhaps we can move on to the reason Mr Laffaye asked me here.' The superintendent glanced around with disdain. He seemed to want to show how unimpressed he was by the luxury of his surroundings. 'A pathologist has examined the body you found at Smugglers Cove. And, as Sergeant Norsworthy has already explained, there's nothing to indicate foul play.'

'How did a man come to die at the foot of a cliff and stay hidden for nearly five years?' Horace enquired politely.

'A coroner will look into the facts.' From his expression, he was determined to impart as little information as possible.

'Doesn't it seem strange to you?' Elijah asked bluntly.

'The circumstances do seem a little odd.' Superintendent Endicott inclined his head to acknowledge this fact.

Odd was an understatement.

'Was anything else found on the body apart from the train ticket? Where was the man's wallet?' I asked. 'Why wasn't it in one of the pockets of his suit or overcoat?'

The superintendent gave a long sigh, then seemed to force himself to answer. 'Nothing else was found in any of the pockets. The suit was made in Belgium.'

'Could this man have been a refugee?' Elijah suggested.

'By the end of the war, eight thousand Belgian refugees had been homed in Devon. I'm sure many suits changed hands in that time.'

'And many refugees have since returned home, presumably taking their suits with them,' Elijah remarked. 'Couldn't it be possible that this man was from Belgium?'

'Mr Rowe's wife did not appear to think it odd that he was wearing the suit. But we will be speaking to her again. I'll also be speaking to Captain and Mrs Keats to see if they can recall anything that might shed some light on the matter.'

'They weren't living at Smugglers Haunt at the time of this man's disappearance.' I noticed Percy and Millicent shift uncomfortably in their seats as I said this.

'Do you happen to know who was living there at the time? You seem to have made it your business to find out a lot about this case,' Superintendent Endicott said dryly.

'Captain Keats' brother, Major Laurence Keats, owned the property. He lived there with his wife, Katherine.'

Elijah's head shot up. 'Katherine lived there?'

I nodded. 'When Major Keats died, his brother, Rupert, inherited Smugglers Haunt.'

The superintendent scribbled this in his pocket book. 'I'll see if I can discover the whereabouts of Mrs Katherine Keats and interview her.'

'She's driving down from Hampshire tomorrow. She'll be staying with her brother, Stephen Damerell, at Primrose Lodge,' I replied.

'I know Mr Damerell. I'll ask him to arrange for me to meet with Mrs Keats.'

Elijah let out a low groan.

* * *

'It's not my fault.'

Elijah gave an exasperated sigh. 'You could have told us about Katherine.'

'I did.'

'I think Mr Whittle meant before we requested the assistance of Superintendent Endicott.' Horace sipped his tea.

After the superintendent had left, Horace suggested to Percy and Millicent that they might like to go and take a look at Exeter Cathedral. My friends had promptly deserted me, Percy grabbing a couple of slices of cake before he went.

'I didn't know until Nathalie Keats told me. Don't you think we should try to find out the truth about this man?'

'We could have delayed talking to the police until after the wedding.' Elijah lit a cigarette. 'The skeleton has been there for a long time. What difference would another two and a half weeks have made?'

'Say Katherine had something to do with it?'

'She didn't,' Elijah growled.

'How do you know?'

He ignored the question. 'How is your father going to feel when he and Katherine arrive in Devon, and she's taken in to be questioned by the police?' Then he added, 'Because of something you told them?'

'It's not my fault,' I said again, aware I sounded childish. 'It wouldn't have taken the superintendent long to find out who was living at Smugglers Haunt at the time the man went missing.'

Horace raised his hand. 'There's no point in arguing now. We'll just have to try to make sure this doesn't cause any ill feeling.'

'I know you're not happy about this wedding.' Elijah waved his cigarette at me. 'But I don't want you to start concocting any wild stories about Katherine.'

'I'm not. I'll explain to Katherine myself when she arrives tomorrow. I'm going to Primrose Lodge with my grandparents to meet her and my father when they arrive.'

'Good.' He eyed me dubiously, then said, 'Go on, off with you. I'm finished with you for the moment.'

But I wasn't finished with him. 'You knew Major Keats, didn't you? Wasn't he your commanding officer for a time?'

'That's right.'

I'd hoped for a bit more than this.

'You met Katherine when you visited her to pay your condolences on the loss of her husband?'

'That's right,' he said again.

It was like getting blood out of a stone. 'When was that?'

'After he died, presumably,' Elijah said sarcastically.

Horace was watching this exchange with a wry smile on his face.

'But when was that?' I asked impatiently.

Elijah screwed up his eyes as if struggling to remember. 'Not long after the war.'

'After the war? Not during?'

'That's what I said.'

'You came to Devon to see Katherine?'

'No. I believe it was in London.'

'Oh.' I considered this. It was possible my father had called on Katherine in London and hadn't told me.

'Any more questions, or can I enjoy my drink in peace?' Elijah gulped back the last of his whisky and soda.

I wasn't done yet. 'The man in the cave had a train ticket dated 10 December 1918, and from what I can ascertain, Laurence Keats died around Christmas time.'

'So?'

'Don't you think it's strange that two men died within weeks of each other in the place where Katherine was living?'

He sighed and reached for his cigarettes.

8

'You've grown since I last saw you.' Stephen Damerell gave me a hug. 'Welcome to the family.'

I may have grown, but at over six foot, he towered above me. I had a vague memory of him visiting us in Walden when I was a child. I wondered if he expected me to call him by some familial name. Not uncle, surely? What did being the brother of a stepmother make you?

'This is my wife, Gwendolen. Call her Gwen – everyone does.'

This was a relief. Evidently, it was going to be Stephen and Gwen rather than some silly title.

'And this is Beatrice and Charles. I'm sure they'd prefer you to call them Bea and Charlie,' Gwen said in a lilting Welsh accent, putting her arms around her two children. While Stephen was tall, dark and lean, she was short, round and fair. Beatrice was a pretty girl of eighteen, who looked like her mother and Charlie an engaging lad of sixteen, who resembled his father.

The Damerells were a friendly bunch, and Primrose Lodge the perfect family home. It smelt of freshly baked bread and fruit cake. The house, an early Victorian pile with crooked chimneys and ivy trailing up the walls, was on Bere Hill in Dawlish, on the outskirts of the Luscombe Castle estate.

In the garden, fragrant rambling roses trailed over an archway and borders were crammed with foxgloves, cranesbill and other wildflowers. A few ancient apple trees dotted the lawn. Bea and Charlie went off to play tennis while Gwen chatted with my grandparents on the patio. The tennis court had seen better days, but that only added to the homely, lived-in feel of the place.

When I went inside to talk to Stephen in his study, I was unsurprised to find an elderly Labrador lolling at his feet. The dog got up to greet me.

'Have a seat.' Stephen gestured to a worn leather armchair. 'You don't mind dogs, do you? Bruno likes to be made a fuss of.'

'Not at all.' I stroked Bruno's ears and he rested his head on my lap. 'I wanted to ask you about the body we found at Smugglers Haunt.'

'Marc told me about that. How are you feeling? It must have been quite frightening.'

'It was fascinating,' I replied. 'It's made me curious to find out who this man was and what happened to him.'

He laughed. 'Katherine warned me about you.'

I wasn't sure what he meant by that and decided it was probably best not to ask. 'My friends and I aren't convinced the police are correct in what they suspect.'

He frowned. 'Arnold Rowe? Yes, that is a bit odd. I've been trying to get hold of him for years.'

'Why?'

'Smugglers Haunt was Laurence Keats' house and should have gone to Katherine after his death. But Laurence added a codicil to his will. When I asked Rupert Keats about it, he told me their father had always stipulated that the house should stay with the male line of the family, and as Laurence and

Katherine didn't have children, Laurence had decided it should go to Rupert.' Stephen rubbed his chin. 'I didn't believe a word of it.'

'What's this got to do with Arnold Rowe?'

'Laurence's signature to the codicil to the will was witnessed by Arnold Rowe and his aunt, Harriet Green, the housekeeper at Smugglers Haunt.'

'When was this?' I was intrigued by how many strange things seemed to have taken place at that picturesque villa.

'Twenty-first of October 1918. Laurence died on the sixteenth of December. I don't believe he was well enough or had any desire to change his will in the months before his death. Yet Harriet Green claims Laurence asked her to witness his signature. Arnold Rowe disappeared before I could get hold of him to see what he had to say about it.'

'Did you know Mr Rowe?'

'Our paths crossed a few times. He was a petty criminal. Mainly importing contraband goods. Nothing too serious. The magistrates around here tend to be lenient if it's only a small amount of liquor and some tobacco.'

'Is that what you think he was doing at the cove?'

'It's possible, although I've never heard of smugglers using that beach in recent years. They know it's private land. And it's not as though they're short of other places to come ashore.'

It didn't sound like Arnold had been there to meet a boat, especially not with a third class return train ticket from Teignmouth in his pocket.

'Mr Rowe lived in Dawlish, didn't he?'

Stephen nodded. 'Yes, with his wife, Joyce.'

'Do you have Mrs Rowe's address? My friend, Millicent, would like to call on his widow to offer her condolences – she was the one who actually uncovered the cave and found the body.' Millicent hadn't mentioned any such thing, but I knew she'd oblige me by going along with it.

'That's kind of her. Let me check.' He went to a filing cabinet and rummaged through some folders. He scribbled down the address on a piece of paper and handed it to me.

'How did Laurence die? I've never liked to ask Katherine.' I had to admit that despite being someone Elijah described as 'inveterately nosy', I'd made little attempt to get to know my future stepmother. Katherine was a forty-five-year-old widower from Devon. That was all I knew about her.

'Poisoned.'

I gasped.

'I know. Grim business. Gassed. Not sure which type. Could have been chlorine or phosgene. Whatever it was, it was a lung irritant. Laurence wasn't even that close to the army base where the gas artillery shells were dropped. But it was his bad luck to get down wind. He started coughing and couldn't stop. He was shipped home. At one point, it looked like he might recover. But alas.' He raised his hands. 'His health deteriorated and he died at the age of forty-nine.'

The same age my father was now. How close had Father come to death when he'd worked with the major? Had he been at this army base when the gas shells were dropped? I'd probably never know. Like Elijah, he refused to talk about his time in the intelligence corps.

'I could have challenged the codicil to the will and won,' Stephen continued. 'But after Laurence's death, Katherine went to live in their flat in London. She was tired and didn't have the will to fight Rupert. She'd been through enough. It still makes me angry. I only tolerate the man for Nathalie's sake.'

'Katherine became acquainted with my father at that time?' I asked.

'I believe so.' He stood up to look out of the window. 'They're here. Let's go out to meet them.'

Did I detect a note of relief in his voice that our conversation was at an end?

I followed him outside and joined in the chorus of greetings. Bea and Charlie rushed forward to hug Katherine, who was clearly delighted to see them. My father put his arm around my shoulder, but his eyes strayed to his future wife. The glance they shared caused me a pang of guilt. Was I about to introduce a sour note into this happy family gathering?

I didn't like myself for the petty resentment I felt towards Katherine. She'd done nothing to deserve it. But whenever I tried to overcome it, she'd do something else to irritate me.

'Good news,' she said when we were seated in the garden. 'Sybil's going to motor down for the wedding. She's bringing Mrs Heathcote with her.'

After my mother's death, Mrs Sybil Siddons, MP, had become my friend and confidante. It niggled me that since Katherine had been spending time in Walden, she and Mrs Siddons had formed a friendship.

I smiled through gritted teeth and told myself not to be childish. After all, I was pleased Mrs Siddons would be at the wedding, I was only feeling peevish because I suspected she gave Katherine advice on how to handle me.

'That will be an adventure for Lizzy,' I replied with a grin. Mrs Elizabeth Heathcote, our housekeeper, hadn't wanted to travel down early with my father and Katherine, fearing she'd be in the way. As she was a great admirer of Mrs Siddons, I suspected she'd leapt at the chance of travelling down with her the day before the wedding. However, I had experience of Mrs Siddons' driving and knew Lizzy would be clutching the sides of her seat for the entire journey.

'Iris has been having some adventures of her own,' Stephen said, reappearing after having carried Katherine's cases to her room. 'She found a skeleton in a cave.'

'It was actually Millicent who found it.' I noticed I was trying to distance myself from the situation. 'The police think it's the body of a local man who went missing about five years ago.'

My father didn't look happy. 'Please don't tell me you've become involved with the local police. Do they want to talk to you?' In his view, Elijah and I had spent far too much time in police company in recent years.

'No. But they'd like to interview Katherine.' I couldn't help myself from saying it.

The shock on my father and Katherine's faces both amused and dismayed me at the same time. I really needed to sort out my feelings about this wedding.

'Me?' Katherine turned to her brother.

'The body was in a cave at Smugglers Cove,' Stephen explained. 'Sergeant Norsworthy thinks it's Arnold Rowe. You remember he went missing in December 1918?'

'Arnold?' Katherine's astonishment seemed genuine. 'He was found at the cove?'

I explained what had happened – how Millicent had been collecting rock samples from the red sandstone cliff to take back for her pupils when there was a rock fall.

'I hope she wasn't hurt,' Katherine said.

'No. She managed to jump out of the way. Did you know about the cave?'

Katherine nodded. 'It was an old fisherman's cave. The entrance to it had become partially blocked over the years. But you could still get into it through a small gap.'

'It seems the entrance was completely blocked.' I didn't

mention Millicent's suspicion that the rocks had been put there on purpose.

'And this man was trapped inside?' Father asked.

Stephen nodded. 'Norsworthy suspects he was up to no good. Arnold Rowe was involved in smuggling. He'd been before the magistrates a few times on charges of bringing in spirits and tobacco from abroad without paying duty.'

Katherine shook her head. 'I can't imagine why he'd want to use Smugglers Cove. The beach and caves are in clear view of the house. I don't ever remember seeing Arnold down there.'

'Did you spend much time on the beach?' I asked.

She smiled. 'I loved the cove. Smugglers Haunt was a wonderful place to live. I was lucky to have spent those years there with Laurence.'

'It should still be yours. That bloody man.'

Stephen was about to continue, but Katherine held up her hand to stop him.

'If Rupert and Nathalie and little Timothy are happy there, then I'm quite content. It's what Laurence would have wanted – to see Rupert settled with his own family.'

Stephen dropped the subject. 'If Superintendent Endicott wants to speak to you, I'll ask him to come here.'

Katherine nodded. 'I don't think there's much I can tell him. Arnold and his wife used to do jobs around the house and garden. I must admit, we all thought Arnold had left to get away from her. Theirs wasn't the most harmonious of marriages. It's strange he was trapped there and no one noticed. I suppose with Laurence being ill at the time, no one visited the beach much.'

After that, Gwen took Katherine upstairs to unpack, and Stephen gave my grandparents a tour of the garden, leaving my father and me alone to chat.

'Why did you go to Smugglers Haunt?' Father's voice was

grave and I didn't like the way he was looking at me. 'Did you know Katherine had once lived there? Were you snooping?'

My nostrils flared. 'It was an accident. What I mean is, we had no idea a house was there or that the beach was private land. Percy heard some tale from his landlady about a smugglers' cove and wanted to visit it. We were paddling in the sea while Millicent collected her rock samples, and that's when it happened.'

I was relieved to see his expression relax. He held up his hands. 'I'm sorry, it's just... sometimes I feel you don't want me to marry Katherine.'

I went to protest but the words didn't come out. I tried again. 'It's not that. It's...' Again, I couldn't find the right words.

'It's your mother, isn't it?'

I nodded. 'I want my mother back. I can't have that. But I don't want her to be replaced. Or forgotten.'

'I could never forget her. And I don't want to. I see her every time I look at you.' He rubbed his eyes.

This made me feel worse. 'It's not your fault. Or Katherine's. I just feel that the more things change, the more Mother fades into the background.'

'Katherine isn't trying to replace her.'

'I know.' *But she is taking her place as your wife*, I thought.

'Katherine's looking forward to your day out together.'

'Me too,' I said untruthfully. I hadn't been looking forward to it at all, although it would give me the opportunity to find out more about Katherine's background.

I hadn't come to Devon with the intention of snooping on Katherine as my father had suggested. But given the events of the last week, it only seemed prudent to do a little investigation into her past.

9

Apart from Stephen and Gwen, Nathalie was the only other person I could think of to ask about Katherine.

Fortunately, Millicent was spending the day at the Royal Albert Memorial Museum in Exeter, so I was able to visit Smugglers Haunt on my own. I could have done with Percy's car, but I wanted to speak to Nathalie alone. So I walked from Primrose Lodge down to Boat Cove and climbed the steps to Lea Mount. I was breathless by the time I came to Teignmouth Road, and when I reached the driveway to Smugglers Haunt, my previously energetic pace had slowed to a weary trudge.

When I heard the noise of a car engine starting, I stepped back into the bushes in case it came at speed towards me.

The sound of raised voices made me stay hidden under the cover of a dense patch of rhododendrons. Two motorcars were parked on the driveway close to the villa.

Emile Vandamme was standing by the door of one, shouting at the driver. 'You were trying to rip us off.'

I craned my head forward and saw that it was Rupert Keats in the driver's seat.

'I didn't know it was the wrong bloody vintage,' he yelled back.

'Then employ someone who knows what they're doing.'

'It won't happen again.' Rupert moved the car forward, causing Emile to jump back.

'You're right, it won't. If this costs me my job, you'll regret it.'

Emile slammed his fist on the roof of Rupert's car before it sped away. Then he jumped into his own car, and after a few false starts, he managed to get the engine going. He drove past me at a much slower speed than Rupert had.

I was about to emerge when I saw a movement. Mrs Green, the housekeeper, was standing in the garden to the side of the house. No doubt, she'd witnessed the exchange.

I gave it another few minutes, waiting for her to go back inside before I approached and rapped on the door. I didn't want to have to explain that I'd been hiding in the bushes. However, the slight nod she gave when she greeted me made me think she'd already been aware of my presence. Without a word, she ushered me through the house and into the garden, where Nathalie was seated on the terrace.

'Iris. How lovely to see you. Mrs Green, could you bring us some lemonade?' She turned back to me. 'You've just missed Emile.'

'I came to see you,' I replied. I guessed Nathalie was used to ladies calling on her as an excuse to get to know her attractive brother. 'I saw him leaving, but he didn't notice me.'

She glanced around. I think to check if Mrs Green was in earshot. 'Were he and Rupert arguing?'

I nodded. 'About some wine?'

'Rupert is not a good businessman. And he's not a good wine merchant. He knows little about the wine he stocks. He supplied some to the hotel where Emile works, but it's not of the quality it should be. Emile becomes frustrated with Rupert's lack of knowledge. I hope Mrs Green didn't hear the row. She is very protective of Rupert.'

I was certain the housekeeper had heard every word of what had been said. 'How is Mrs Green?' I asked.

Nathalie wrinkled her nose. 'Not her usual self. She's not happy. She seems to have accepted that the body is that of her nephew, Arnold.'

I was surprised at this and wondered what had convinced her. When Mrs Green appeared with a tray bearing a jug of lemonade and two glasses, her expression dissuaded me from asking.

Instead, I diplomatically changed the subject and made polite conversation about the garden. 'What an unusual rose.'

I'd spotted it as soon as I'd sat down. It wasn't like any rose I'd seen before. It had full pink flowers that were unevenly striped with fuchsia, magenta and white. It looked like someone had shaken a paintbrush and covered it with streaks of colour.

Nathalie smiled. 'It's new. It was bred in France only a couple of years ago. The cultivar is called Ferdinand Pichard. I was visiting my godmother in Paris shortly after Timothy was born, and she gave it to me. It's so beautiful and dramatic. It has pride of place. Smell it.'

I leant forward and breathed in a rich, fruity fragrance. 'It's heavenly.'

'The flowers are at their best in July and August.' Nathalie poured out two glasses of cloudy lemonade. 'This is not how we make lemonade in my country. But I have come to like the English way. It's Rupert's favourite. Mrs Green has made it for him since he was a child. She came to Smugglers Haunt as a young woman to work for Rupert's parents.'

'And she was housekeeper for Major Keats when he lived here?'

She nodded. 'She's been here forever. She's very loyal to the Keats family.'

A thought occurred to me that Arnold Rowe may not have been as loyal to the Keats family as his aunt. Perhaps he threatened to tell the truth about witnessing Major Keats' signature to the will. Had Rupert Keats retaliated and shut him up?

'I suspect she's a little put out that Katherine is getting married again. She can be funny about things like that,' Nathalie continued. 'I think it's wonderful that Katherine has found someone to be happy with again. Are you looking forward to the wedding?'

'It's what I came to talk to you about,' I said, avoiding answering the question directly. 'I realise I don't know much about Katherine. Perhaps you could tell me about her. You said you were fond of her?'

'She was kind to Annette and me when we arrived in Devon. Many people were kind, but it was so nice to talk to someone who could speak our language. We are Dutch speakers. She helped us to complete the paperwork we needed and found us a place to live.'

'You became friends?'

She nodded. 'Katherine arranged for us to board with Dr Frampton and his wife. The surgery is part of their house and Dr Frampton gave me a job as his receptionist.'

'You lived with them during the war?'

'They are good people. I stayed with them until I married Rupert. When Emile and Marc returned to us in November 1918, it took a while to sort out somewhere permanent for them to live. After Marc found a flat in Exeter and Annette moved out of the surgery to be with him, Emile took her room. He's been living with the Framptons ever since.'

'Why did you all decide to stay here and not return to Belgium?'

Nathalie sighed. 'Annette lost everyone. Her parents died before the war so her brother and uncle were all she had. Both were shot by the Germans. Thank goodness Marc had the sense to marry her before we left Belgium, otherwise she would have been alone.'

I shuddered at the horror.

'You can understand why she and Marc chose not to go back. Emile and I decided to stay too. We'd all been through so much together. Annette is like a sister to me. If things had worked out, she would have been my sister. I was in love with her brother and wanted us to marry before I left Belgium. But my parents wouldn't allow it. So we promised we would wait until the war ended.' Tears filled her eyes. 'I waited in vain. But I thank God every day for the safe return of Emile and Marc. And for the kind people who helped us. First Katherine and the Framptons, then you and your grandmother for reuniting us, and Stephen and Gwen for helping Marc and Emile to find jobs.'

'All I did was write to my grandmother,' I remarked.

'You cared for them when they were in London.' She smiled at me. 'I'd like to thank you all. I'm going to hold a dinner party here to celebrate the joining together of your father and Katherine. Emile will do the cooking. It will also be an opportunity to wish Marc and Annette well in their new life.'

'New life?'

'They're moving to London. Emile and I are going to miss them so much. You will come, won't you? Your friends won't be offended if I don't invite them? I can't fit more than twelve guests around the table.'

I assured her they wouldn't mind and asked who would make up the other dinner guests.

'Your father and Katherine, Marc and Annette, your grandparents, Stephen and Gwen, me and Rupert. And Emile will be your escort,' she said with a wink.

I felt myself blush. However, I didn't demur. I was sure Emile would make an extremely entertaining escort.

'How did you and Rupert meet?' I asked.

'Rupert had been honourably discharged from the army and was living above his shop in Exeter. He was here often, looking after Laurence. And he frequently visited Dr Frampton's surgery to pick up Laurence's medication. He began to woo me.' She frowned. 'That is the correct word? Woo? It is a very strange word.'

I smiled. 'It is a funny word. My friend, Millicent, would probably know where it came from.'

'When he first asked me to marry him, I turned him down. I told him I'd promised someone back home that I would wait for him until the war ended. That was not to be, so on Armistice Day when Rupert asked me to marry him again, I said yes. He told me he would soon inherit Smugglers Haunt and that it was his dream that we should live here together.' She smiled as she looked around the garden. 'Who could resist this?'

So he'd promised her they would live at Smugglers Haunt a month before his brother had died and only weeks after the codicil had been added to the will. It sounded as if she'd been wooed by the house rather than by Rupert.

'Are you happy here?'

'It is not all roses.' She indicated the strange pink flowers with her delicate white hand. 'That is a good phrase, is it not? Life cannot be all roses. Although Rupert tries hard, his business is not as successful as we would like. And he and Emile have never got on. But we have Timmy and our kind English friends. So, I cannot complain.'

I wondered how Katherine would feel about revisiting the house where she'd lived with her first husband accompanied by her future husband. She said she'd hoped Smugglers Haunt would give Rupert a stable family life, and it sounded like it had.

But I couldn't help thinking that to give away a house was an extremely magnanimous gesture. And from what she'd said, it had been a house that she'd loved and held happy memories.

Was it possible there was another reason for Katherine choosing not to fight the codicil Stephen believed had been added illegally to Laurence Keats' will?

10

The following day, Millicent and I took the train to Dawlish and on our way to Mrs Rowe's home on Barton Crescent, we enjoyed a leisurely stroll along the brook. Without Percy and his toast, the black swans ignored us.

It was a little too early to pay a call, so we visited the nearby parish church of St Michael's and All Angels, where the wedding would be held in two weeks' time.

'It's beautiful.' Millicent sighed. 'If I ever get married, I'd like it to be in a church like this.'

It was lovely. A traditional church surrounded by picturesque Devonshire countryside. The inside was as charming as the exterior, the altar decorated with flowers and ribbons in preparation for a wedding that afternoon. It was very different to St Stephen's Church in Lewisham, where my father and mother had married.

'The sandstone tower is mediaeval,' Millicent informed me. 'The rest of the church was mostly rebuilt in the last century.'

I stared at the altar where the happy couple would exchange vows and felt like crying. My father would be committing to a new future with Katherine, and his old life with my mother would fade even further into the past.

I left Millicent admiring the ornate stone pulpit and went outside to wander amongst the gravestones. Reading some of the inscriptions brought home the fragility of life, as did the granite cross war memorial. How many times had I been thankful that Father had come home to me when thousands of other men hadn't returned to their families? I wiped away a tear, knowing I should be grateful that he'd found someone he could be happy with.

Millicent appeared at my side. Without saying anything, she linked her arm through mine, and we left the churchyard.

Mrs Rowe lived in the ground floor flat of a terraced house on Barton Crescent.

'Mrs Damerell said you'd call. Go into the parlour, and I'll make tea.'

We sat on a small sofa, and I noticed a cushioned upright chair close to the bay window that looked out onto the road. I got the impression Mrs Rowe liked to watch the goings-on of her neighbours.

'We wanted to offer our condolences,' Millicent said when Mrs Rowe returned with a tea tray. 'You know we found your husband's body?'

She nodded. 'Call me Joyce. It must have been horrible for you. Finding him like that.' She placed a large brown teapot on a lace doily in the centre of a round occasional table, then set out three rose-patterned china teacups and saucers.

'It wasn't pleasant,' Millicent admitted. 'Do you have any idea what he might have been doing in the cave?'

Joyce Rowe had dyed blonde hair and high narrow cheekbones that made her large blue eyes appear too big for her face. She gave a sigh and adopted the expression of a long-suffering wife. 'I'm afraid Arnold was, well, what you might call a bit of a villain. Nothing nasty. But he was always getting involved in some scheme or another. He could be a bit gullible at times.'

'You think someone took advantage of him?' Millicent asked.

'I don't know what to think. Sergeant Norsworthy probably has more idea about what Arnold was up to than I do. Or his aunt. She works up at Smugglers Haunt. He used to spend more time up there than he did here.' She didn't bother to hide her resentment.

'I thought you worked there too?' I said.

Joyce bridled at this. 'I helped out. When the major was so ill, I felt it was my duty. But I didn't spend as much time there as Arnold did.'

She made it sound as though she was doing the Keats a favour rather than being employed as a cleaner. It was interesting that she wanted to distance herself from Smugglers Haunt.

'Did you know anything about the codicil added to Major Keats' will?' I asked. 'Your husband witnessed the major's signature.'

'Mr Damerell asked me about that. Arnold didn't mention it to me. I reckon it was his aunt's doing. He'd do whatever she told him.'

'Mrs Green was shocked when she found out it was the body of her nephew we'd found in the cave,' Millicent said pointedly.

Joyce looked sheepish. 'I should have gone to see her, but I thought she knew. What with her living at Smugglers Haunt.'

'This must have come as a great shock to both of you,' Millicent said in a gentler tone.

Joyce dabbed at her eyes with a handkerchief, but I couldn't see any tears. 'We both thought he'd run off, though I was surprised that he didn't even show his face at Christmas. Arnold and I hadn't been getting on too well. We were young when we married. I should have listened to my mother. She told me I was too good for him.'

I wondered if Joyce's mother could be considered a suspect. 'Mr Rowe was wearing a brown tweed suit and grey woollen overcoat. Do you remember those items? The pathologist seemed to think the suit had been made in Belgium.'

She shook her head. 'I can't recall. Arnold was always trading with someone. This place was full of refugees during the war. He probably got some clothes off one of them.'

'Did Arnold have a wedding ring?' I asked.

She bristled at this. 'Of course he did.'

'What was it like?'

She regarded me with suspicion, as if I was trying to catch her out. 'A plain gold band. Why?'

'The one he was wearing wasn't like that.'

She made a humph sound. 'He probably pawned it, knowing Arnold.'

I noticed she wasn't wearing a wedding ring either and was tempted to ask if she'd pawned hers too. 'The one he was wearing was silver and engraved with doves.'

Colour rose to her cheeks. 'I don't know anything about that. He certainly didn't get it from me.'

'Where do you think he got it from?' I poured a little more milk into the strong dark tea she'd handed me.

'Like I said, he'd trade anything with anyone. Though he probably got it from a woman. I don't like to speak ill of the dead, but Arnold was a wrong'un. He liked ciggies, booze, getting one over on the law, and cheap tarts.' She spat these last words.

'That must have been very trying for you,' Millicent said sympathetically.

'It was.' Mrs Rowe seemed mollified by this. 'But I'm a Christian woman, and I was true to my wedding vows. Till death us do part. And now I'm a widow.'

And not a grieving one by the slight note of triumph I detected in her voice. I tried to adopt Millicent's concerned tone. 'Has a death certificate been issued?'

'Not yet.' She pursed her thin lips. 'There's going to be an inquest. Lord knows how long that will take.'

Mrs Rowe seemed in a hurry to proclaim her husband dead and take on the official mantle of widowhood. Yet I wondered if she really did believe the body in the cave was Arnold.

Millicent made sympathetic noises and offered a few more words of comfort before we took our leave.

'Did you get the impression she was glad to be rid of her husband?' I was aware of Joyce watching us from her upright chair by the window as we walked along Barton Crescent. 'A little too keen for the body to be his?'

'If it's not him, who could it be?' Millicent replied.

'I'm puzzled by the ring. Surely someone would have noticed if Arnold Rowe had taken to wearing it. Especially in place of his wedding band.'

'Mrs Green would be the best person to ask. Shall we pay a visit to Smugglers Haunt?'

* * *

Millicent and I walked down to the seafront and along to Boat Cove. I warned her about the steep climb as we took the steps up to Lea Mount.

When we reached the top, I noticed how far back the villa was set from the Teignmouth Road. It wouldn't be visible from any cars travelling along the road as it was further down the cliff. If smuggling were going on at the cove, it would make sense for the goods to be moved through the house and into a vehicle on the driveway. Anyone attempting to bring goods up via the public footpath would end up in the lay-by in full view of passing motorists.

The front door of Smugglers Haunt was answered by Annette Jansen. We explained that we'd come to see Mrs Green.

'I believe she's gone into town. Nathalie is in the garden. Come, she will be pleased to see you.'

We followed Annette through the house to the terrace, where Nathalie was playing with Timothy.

'I don't believe Mrs Green will be long if you'd like to wait,' Nathalie said when we told her the reason for our visit. 'Have you found out something more about Mr Rowe?'

'We've been to see his widow to offer our condolences,' Millicent said, taking the chair Annette proffered.

'She must be very upset.' Annette sat beside Timothy and stroked the little boy's blond head as he played with his new train.

Millicent and I exchanged a glance. Nathalie must have caught the look as she asked. 'Is that not the case? Is Mrs Rowe not the grieving widow?'

'To be frank, she almost seemed too keen for it to be her husband.'

Nathalie shrugged. 'That is not so strange. If he's been missing for five years, it must be a relief to know for certain what has happened to him.'

Annette nodded in agreement, her huge brown eyes filled with compassion. 'It is hard when you have no news of your loved ones.'

'From what we've learnt, there seems to have been little love lost between the Rowes,' I said.

Nathalie nodded. 'Mrs Green told me she was shocked it was

Arnold because she'd always believed he'd run away from his wife.'

'Mrs Rowe thought the same, and I got the impression she wasn't sorry when he went,' I commented. 'She said he liked booze and women and didn't always stay on the right side of the law.'

Nathalie looked thoughtful. 'She wouldn't have been able to divorce him on the grounds of his infidelity alone, would she?'

'Those laws are soon to change, are they not?' Annette said with enthusiasm.

'Yes, they are,' I replied, surprised by the turn of the conversation.

'We've been reading about Mrs Siddons in the newspapers,' Nathalie explained. 'Katherine tells us that she's coming to the wedding. I am very excited to meet her.'

For some time, Mrs Siddons had been campaigning for reforms to divorce laws. Currently, a husband could petition for a divorce from his wife if he had proof of her infidelity. However, a husband committing adultery was not considered sufficient grounds for a wife to apply for a divorce – it had to be aggravated by another matrimonial offence, such as cruelty or desertion of two years. Mrs Siddons had recently been successful in her campaign to change the law to put men and women on a more equal footing.

'A woman will be able to divorce her adulterous husband, is that not so?' Annette asked eagerly.

'Yes, although she would need to offer the court proof,' I explained.

Annette nodded gravely. 'Of course.'

I couldn't help thinking that Nathalie and Annette were well informed on the subject of divorce law. From what Nathalie had told me, Annette was completely dependent on Marc. Even if he was unfaithful, I couldn't imagine her giving up the security he offered and seeking a divorce. However, Nathalie was a much stronger character. She was clearly the more dominant of the two women. If she'd tired of the much older Rupert, would she contemplate life as a divorced woman? It wasn't an easy option, especially for someone from a different country.

Before I could ask any questions, Mrs Green came out to the terrace. She seemed surprised to see Millicent and me. And not too happy.

'I didn't realise you had visitors, Mrs Keats,' she said primly.

'Iris and Millicent are here to see you. Why don't you come and sit down.' Nathalie stood up and offered the housekeeper her own seat. 'Timmy has been begging us to play bowls with him.'

At this, the boy leapt up from his chair, taking his mother's outstretched hand. Annette obediently followed the pair over to the lawn, and I noticed how in control Nathalie was – very much mistress of the house.

Mrs Green hesitated but was left with little choice but to take the chair Nathalie had vacated.

'I'm sorry to trouble you,' Millicent said. 'I wanted to apologise for upsetting you the other day. It was thoughtless of me not to consider that Mr Rowe might have relatives who hadn't yet been informed of events.'

'It's not your fault.' Mrs Green seemed to relax a little. 'I was upset with Sergeant Norsworthy and Joyce for not bothering to tell me they thought it was Arnold.'

'We called on Mrs Rowe this morning to offer our condolences,' Millicent said.

Mrs Green pursed her lips but said nothing.

'She didn't seem too upset,' I commented.

'I bet she told you that she was too good for Arnold. Well, it was the other way around. She trapped him. Couldn't wait to get a ring on her finger. Then as soon as she had it, she started to say she could have done better. And I think she started to look around too.'

Millicent gave the same sympathetic nod she'd used on Joyce Rowe.

I wanted to ask Mrs Green about the codicil added to the will in October 1918. In particular, whether Rupert Keats had persuaded her and Arnold to witness Laurence Keats' signature. Had it been obtained under duress? Or had Rupert forged it? But it was a difficult subject to broach with Nathalie and Annette nearby. Although they'd discreetly left us on the pretext of playing bowls with Timothy, their lack of conversation suggested they were listening to our every word.

Instead, I said, 'You seemed surprised that the body we found was Mr Rowe. Did Sergeant Norsworthy satisfy your doubts?'

Mrs Green shrugged. 'Joyce seems to think it was him. And I suppose she'd know.'

'Perhaps she recognised his wedding ring.' I improvised. 'It was quite distinctive.'

Her brow creased. 'Arnold had a plain gold wedding band. I presume she'd have recognised any markings on it.'

'The ring on the man's wedding finger was silver. It was engraved with tiny doves. Do you remember if he was wearing it before he went missing?'

She shook her head. 'I can't say I recall what he was wearing the last time I saw him. Or what day it was. There wasn't much that needed doing in the garden at that time of the year. I remember Mrs Keats wanting the windows to be cleaned and he came over and did them. I think that must have been the last time he was here. Joyce came in every other day, and it was close to Christmas when she told me she hadn't seen Arnold for a couple of weeks.'

'Do you remember who called at the house during December?' I asked.

'I don't keep a diary. Mr and Mrs Damerell visited regularly. Captain Keats came most days, particularly if he knew Mrs Keats wouldn't be around and Major Keats would be on his own.'

'Where was Mrs Keats?' It was a presumptuous question, but one I couldn't resist asking.

Mrs Green sniffed. 'She spent a lot of time in London. Even when her husband was dying.'

'Why?'

'War work.'

'I thought Major Keats died after the war ended?'

'That's right.' Mrs Green's tone left me in no doubt as to what she thought of Katherine leaving her husband's sickbed to go to London. 'Apparently there were still reports that needed to be filed with the relevant authorities.'

'I see,' I replied. But I didn't see. What could have been so important that Katherine had left her dying husband's bedside to go to London?

11

On Saturday, Millicent and I walked from Dawlish railway station to Marine Parade and called at the Jewel of the Sea guest house.

Emerald Dubois appeared, wrapped in a bright green silk kimono. She welcomed us with a theatrical wave of her arm, sending wafts of orange blossom perfume in our direction. It was overlaid with the scent of alcohol and sweat. 'Percy's in the lounge. Come through.' She ushered us into a front room that offered a view of the railway line.

Percy was lying full-length on a green velvet couch reading the June edition of *Picturegoer*. The actress, Lilian Hall-Davis, smiled from the front cover, holding a sprig of spring flowers.

Emerald made a great show of introducing Dame Cicely Campbell and Mr Gordon Andrews, who were seated at a card table playing a game of cribbage. 'They're starring in *The Second Mrs Tanqueray* at the Theatre Royal in Exeter.'

Dame Cicely inclined her head towards us. 'I play Mrs Cortelyon, a small but essential part.'

Mr Andrews got to his feet and bowed. 'And I play Frank Misquith, a genial fellow who likes a drink.'

Judging by Mr Andrews' demeanour and the glasses of gin on the card table, the role wasn't much of a stretch for him. He was about fifty years old with a red face and a thick moustache that far surpassed Percy's whiskers. It even curled up at the ends. His hair was dyed a rich chestnut brown, as was the moustache, while Dame Cicely's curls were as unlikely a shade of gold as Emerald's shiny copper locks.

The lounge was decorated with old theatre posters and photographs taken from Emerald's days on the stage. In one, she appeared to be dressed as Cleopatra. A mahogany bar enclosed the corner of the room surrounded by barstools.

'The show runs for another two weeks. Why don't you come with us to see it? Percy's going to take me in his motorcar.' She winked at Percy and propped herself up on one of the stools.

'That sounds fun.' Millicent gamely joined Emerald at the bar.

'We wouldn't want to intrude on your date.' I smirked, hopping onto a stool next to Millicent.

Emerald laughed. 'You can make sure he behaves himself. I've got my reputation to think of.' She curled one of her red locks around her finger.

'I would be happy to escort you all,' Percy said gallantly, then quickly changed the subject. 'Did you call on Mrs Rowe yesterday? I hope she wasn't too upset.'

'Not exactly,' I replied.

'She didn't come across as a grieving widow,' Millicent commented.

'I bet she didn't.' Emerald reached across the bar for a bottle of gin and poured a healthy slug into a shot glass. 'Arnie was too good for her. She's happy he's dead.'

'Why do you say that?' Millicent asked.

'She's been seeing Fred Pike, the ironmonger. He's older than her, but it's his own business, and he does a good trade.' She took a swig of gin. 'I can't blame her. She's been stuck on her own since Arnie went. Without knowing if he was dead or alive, she couldn't snare Fred. But now she's got her sights on marriage.' She waved her glass in our direction. 'Can I get you one?'

Millicent and I declined the offer. Percy rose from the couch, hopped onto the barstool beside her, and poured a shot.

'Did you know Mr Rowe well?' I asked.

'Arnie was a lovely man. I can't believe he's gone.' Emerald sniffed. 'He stayed here sometimes. When he was on business.'

Millicent looked confused. 'He lived in Dawlish, didn't he? With Mrs Rowe in Barton Crescent?'

'It wasn't the sort of business he wanted her to know about.'

'Smuggling,' Percy announced.

At this, Dame Cicely and Mr Andrews clinked their glasses in a toast. 'Smuggling!' they chorused.

Emerald giggled. 'Shhhh. I don't want the other guests to hear. And I don't want any trouble with Norsworthy.'

'Man's an idiot.' Percy leant towards Emerald and said conspiratorially. 'Can I show them what you showed me?'

Emerald giggled again and glanced at him from under her lashes.

Millicent shot me an alarmed look. I smiled and shrugged. I had no idea what they were talking about.

'Go on then.' Emerald winked. 'But not a word to anyone.'

We followed Percy out of the room into the hallway.

'Is Cicely really a dame?' Millicent whispered.

Percy laughed. 'She acts like one, though I believe the king has yet to bestow that honour upon her.'

He led us to the rear of the house.

Marine Parade had been built directly in front of the red sandstone cliff, and it was strange to find ourselves in a tiny yard with such a majestic backdrop. Millicent pointed to the small cave-like indentations similar to the ones we saw at Smugglers Cove.

Percy beckoned us to follow him into what looked like an outdoor privy. 'It's not what you think.'

'I'm glad to hear it,' I replied.

He opened the wooden door into what turned out to be a small shed. Shrimping nets hung on hooks along a shelf at the back. Millicent and I watched as Percy looped his finger through one of the hooks and pulled. The back panel of the shed swung open like a door.

Crouching low, Percy led the way into a cave that was similar in construct to the one at Smugglers Cove. The smooth walls and vaulted roof had been enlarged by hand, and the entrance strengthened by stone walling. This cave was much larger than the one at the cove, around twenty-four feet deep by about twelve feet high.

Millicent examined the walls. 'Another fisherman's cellar. A boat was probably stored in this one. It's large enough.'

I peered into one of the wooden crates that were stacked at the rear of the cave and pulled out a bottle of French brandy. 'It's not being used to store boats any more.'

'Emerald says it was used by smugglers, and it's only right that she keeps up the tradition.' Percy grinned. 'Damn fine brandy.'

'Did she get this stuff from Arnold Rowe?' I asked.

He shook his head. 'Emerald hasn't seen him since he disappeared. But she's on good terms with some of his colleagues.'

'And she gets this stuff from them?'

He nodded. 'She lets them use this place to hide contraband goods in exchange for a few bottles and cigarettes.'

'Probably more than a few.' I examined the stacks of wooden crates.

'She likes to keep her guests entertained. These theatrical types enjoy a drop of the hard stuff.'

I guessed that was why Percy was so enamoured of his lodgings.

'They bring this in by boat from across the channel?' Millicent poked around in one of the crates and pulled out a box of cigars. 'And don't pay duty at any ports?'

'That's right. It's not the business it once was, but they still do a few crossings every so often.'

'Where do the boats land?' I asked.

'Coryton Cove and sometimes in the bay close to Langstone Rock at Dawlish Warren. The coastguards turn a blind eye in exchange for a few bottles.'

'And all the stuff is stored here?' I gazed at the crates, which were stacked up to five high in places.

'It is now.'

'Where was it stored before?'

'There are similar caves in the cliffs under the Mount Pleasant Inn at the warren. According to Emerald, it used to be big business. Smugglers supplied taverns all around the district. The war put an end to it. Nowadays, she says it's just a small amount of contraband for locals to enjoy.'

It didn't look like a small amount to me. The locals must be a thirsty bunch.

'Was the landlord of the Mount Pleasant involved?' Millicent asked.

'Emerald made it sound as though he was one of the organisers. Not any more, though. His name's Owen Locke, and it seems he and Emerald have had words. It's too risky for him to sell contraband these days. And giving cheap stuff to the locals is bad for his business.'

'Did he know Arnold Rowe?' I took a last look at the stack of crates, wondering if Emerald was supplying more than just locals, then headed back into the shed. The earthy smell of the rocks was replaced by the fishy odour from the shrimping nets.

Percy followed me out. 'Oh yes. Apparently, Arnold used to go out in the boats.'

'Shall we go for a drink at the Mount Pleasant?' I suggested.

Percy beamed. 'Super idea.'

12

The following morning, Millicent and I got off the train at Dawlish Warren and spotted Percy's Ford parked in the motorcar enclosure.

We wandered up to the seafront and found Percy sitting on the sea wall watching the holidaymakers. It was a clear day. To the left, you could see across the estuary to Exmouth, and to the right, the headland known as Langstone Rock and Dawlish beyond.

We walked alongside the sea wall, then descended some steps to the curve of beach at the foot of Langstone Rock. Children with nets were catching crabs in the rock pools, and Percy couldn't resist joining them. He pointed out some black sea urchins, explaining that they could sting. Millicent and I sat on the dry sand high up the beach and watched.

'I've been thinking about Joyce Rowe. I wonder when she started seeing Fred Pike, the ironmonger.'

'You suspect her?' Millicent was wide-eyed. 'I know she wasn't upset by his death, but that doesn't mean she murdered him.'

'She worked as a cleaner at Smugglers Haunt. Mrs Green said

she came to the villa every other day. If Arnold was involved in something down at the cave, she might have known about it.'

'You think Joyce killed him because of Fred Pike?'

'Not just that. If Joyce spotted the silver ring on Arnold's finger, it could have been the last straw if she thought it had been given to him by "one of his floozies", as she put it. She'd had enough of their marriage – and Fred Pike could have started sniffing around by then.'

'I'm not sure she'd have been able to shift those boulders. I suppose it's possible.'

'Katherine said she remembered the cave being partially blocked but you could still get into it through a gap. If not many rocks were needed to fill the hole, perhaps a woman could have done it.'

'Nathalie couldn't possibly have moved those rocks.' Percy flopped down on the sand beside us. It hadn't taken long for him to get his trousers soaked.

'We weren't talking about Nathalie.' I explained my theory about Joyce Rowe.

'They do say it's always the one closest to the victim.' He stretched out his long legs, trying to dry his trousers in the sun. 'Though she would have had to have known about the cave.'

Millicent gazed out to sea at the assortment of boats on the water. Then she stood up to scrutinise the cliffs behind us. 'It makes more sense to land a boat here than at Smugglers Cove, even though you still have to cross the railway line.' She motioned with her arm. 'All this open space, and it's flat. It would be easy to unload your goods and pile them into a cart. They could be hidden in the cliff caves or moved by road.'

'The Mount Pleasant Inn is up there.' Percy pointed to the top of the cliff. 'If the caves are directly beneath it, they'll be over there somewhere.'

'You'd just need to take the goods over the railway line and hide them in the caves. You could retrieve them at night when it's quiet with little risk of being seen.'

Percy looked up at Millicent. 'Have you thought of becoming a smuggler? I think you'd be very good at it.'

She laughed. 'Come on. Let's walk up to the pub.'

'Here's an idea.' Percy stood up and flapped his wide trouser legs around in the breeze. 'The cave could have been used for romantic trysts. Perhaps Arnold and Joyce would meet there when they were courting. Then, as the marriage soured, Arnold started to meet other ladies there. Joyce caught him at it and bashed him over the head with a rock.'

I stood up and brushed sand from my skirt. 'Another thought is that Arnold was using the cave to hide stolen goods rather than anything smuggled in by boat.'

Millicent nodded. 'The landlord of the Mount Pleasant might know what Arnold was up to.'

We left the warren and walked up the steep incline of Mount Pleasant Road to the inn perched at the top of the hill.

'I'm famished.' Percy panted. 'I hope this place does food.'

'I bet you ate an enormous cooked breakfast,' I said.

'Sea air makes me hungry.'

It was Sunday and the pub was packed with locals inside and holidaymakers outside. We managed to find a table at the far end of the garden, which offered sea views of Dawlish Warren and the Exe Estuary.

Percy went inside to order a plate of sandwiches and three glasses of lemonade. He admitted he couldn't face a beer after enjoying too much of Emerald's brandy the night before.

'There's a large chap inside that could be Owen Locke. But I didn't get a chance to speak to him.'

When a young woman brought out our sandwiches and

lemonade, Percy asked if she'd pass on a message – that we'd be grateful if Mr Locke could spare us a few minutes for a private chat.

We took our time eating lunch. After an hour, we'd finished the sandwiches and drinks, and there was still no sign of the landlord.

'Should we go in and ask for him?' Millicent suggested.

Percy shook his head. 'I wouldn't recommend it. The locals stare at you as if you're going to murder their grannies. Very suspicious lot. They'd eavesdrop on any conversation. Best try to get him out here. Let's wait until this crowd has gone.'

We saw some of the locals leave, and the garden began to clear, the lunchtime rush now over. By the time the landlord appeared, we had our corner of the garden to ourselves.

'You wanted a word?' Owen Locke was a muscular man with cropped grey hair and a face that looked like he'd spent years at sea in all weathers. He had a huge black dog of indeterminate breed at his heel.

'I'm Percy Baverstock, and I'm staying at the Jewel of the Sea boarding house in Dawlish. These are my friends, Miss Woodmore and Miss Nightingale. I hope you don't mind, but we'd like to ask you about Arnold Rowe.'

'Why?' he asked bluntly.

'Miss Dubois told me in confidence that you used to participate in the time-honoured traditions of these parts,' Percy said with a wink. 'She still keeps up the old ways, and kindly let me sample some of her goods.'

'Aren't you the lucky one.' Owen grinned, his pale blue eyes crinkling.

Percy reddened and hastened to clarify what he meant. 'Her brandy, I mean.'

'You looking for any sort in particular?'

'That French cognac was rather good...'

I decided Percy was making a hash of this so I took over. 'We found Arnold Rowe's body at Smugglers Cove.'

Owen nodded. 'I heard about that.'

'Do you have any idea why he would have been there?'

'Would he have been meeting a boat?' Percy enquired. 'It was just before Christmas. A few spirits to keep the locals warm?'

'We packed up during the war.' Owen turned to walk away.

'Mr Locke,' Millicent said a tone she sometimes used to address her pupils. 'We're not interested in any illegal activities you may have been involved in. I found the body in the cave, and I want to know if that poor man really is Arnold Rowe.'

Owen Locke turned to scrutinise her. Then he put the glasses back on the table and sat down.

'It's an odd one. Smugglers Cove hasn't been used for centuries. Back then, excisemen patrolled the coast, and the coves towards Teignmouth offered more privacy. Smugglers had to be more careful on this side of Dawlish. In those days, the landlord here would put lanterns in the windows to indicate which side of the estuary was safe that night. Smugglers would hide on the warren until it was clear. They stored the goods in the old fisherman's caves in the cliffs below the inn.'

'What about this century?' Millicent asked. 'Did smuggling go on before the war?'

He nodded. 'We had quite a business going, but that all ended years ago. We never used Smugglers Cove, though.'

'What about now? The tradition hasn't died out completely,' Percy said with another unnecessary wink.

'I spent nearly four years in the navy. When the war was over, I'd had enough of ships. I'd turned forty and was too old to go back to that game. It had got too dangerous. I know the odd boat brings stuff in now and again, and I turn a blind eye to a little bit of duty-free for the locals, but I come down on anything more than that – otherwise I'd be out of business.'

'You knew Arnold Rowe?' I prompted.

He nodded. 'He came out on the boats with me a few times. But he didn't have the stomach for it.' He gave a short laugh. 'He was better on land, doing the legwork. Distributing the goods.'

Percy scratched his head. 'So you're saying nothing was going on when Arnold Rowe went missing in December 1918?'

Owen shook his head. 'Not to my knowledge.'

'Did you know there was a cave at Smugglers Cove?' Millicent asked.

'Given the name, it doesn't come as a huge surprise. There are caves all along the coast.'

'Did Arnold know about it?'

The black dog was becoming impatient and started to whine. I ruffled his ears and he lolled to the ground at my feet.

'Probably. His aunt works at the house, and he used to do odd jobs there.'

'Rupert Keats spent a lot of time at Smugglers Haunt. Could he and Arnold have cooked something up together?' I suggested.

'It's possible.' He rubbed his stubbly chin. 'Arnie could be gullible. Keats might have talked him into something.'

'A bigger smuggling operation? More than just a few bottles for the locals?' I wanted to know what had caused the rift between Owen and Emerald.

He nodded. 'Keats came here one night and started asking me about the boats. He said he'd heard we used to bring in a fair amount of liquor. I told him what I've told you. Those days are long gone. But he was persistent. I knew what he was after – but I told him to get lost.'

'What was he after?' I asked.

'Illegal stock. He wanted me to supply him with contraband

booze for his shop, which he'd sell at full price to his customers. Man's an idiot. It would only take one bottle to fall into the hands of someone who knows about the provenance of these things, and we'd be up on a charge. I wasn't about to take stupid risks to line his pockets.' He jerked his head back towards the pub. 'My business is clean. The days of selling dodgy booze and fags are long gone. He might have talked Elsie into putting a few crates his way, but he didn't get anything from me.'

'Elsie?' Percy looked puzzled.

'Your landlady. Emerald Dubois or whatever she calls herself now. She'll always be Elsie Dobson around here.'

Millicent and I sniggered.

Owen stood up and picked up the empty glasses. 'Arnold could have been stupid enough to try to bring a boat into Smugglers Cove. But it would have been a risky thing to do on his own. And he'd have had to have taken the goods through the house, Smugglers Haunt. It would have been damned near impossible to get them up that cliff any other way.'

'Thank you, Mr Locke,' Millicent said. 'We appreciate your honesty.'

He nodded and strolled back into the pub, the black dog at his heels.

'I don't believe Arnold could have transported contraband goods through Smugglers Haunt without anyone noticing. Someone living there had to have been involved.'

Percy sighed. 'You're not suggesting Katherine is a smuggler?'

'I was thinking about Rupert Keats. It sounds like he was there most days when his brother was ill. And Katherine was away for some of that time. If what Stephen suspects is true, he roped Arnold into falsely declaring he'd witnessed the major's signature to the codicil to the will. He could also have persuaded him to start smuggling again.'

Millicent appeared thoughtful. 'Do you think Emerald is supplying Rupert Keats with smuggled wine and spirits?'

'Elsie,' I corrected with a grin.

Percy looked sheepish. 'You know that morning we went to Smugglers Haunt, and I told you Rupert wouldn't be there because I'd seen him in town?'

'Yes.' I eyed him curiously.

'It was because he was at the boarding house.'

'With Emerald?'

Percy nodded. 'I thought he was at the Jewel of the Sea for other reasons. Emerald is a friendly lady.'

'You thought he'd been up to something with her? But that something might not have been what you assumed it was?'

'Yes. That about sums it up,' Percy agreed.

'Or it could have been exactly what you thought,' Millicent said.

'True. I wouldn't like to speculate,' Percy said gallantly.

'Nathalie and Annette seem well versed in the recent change in divorce laws concerning adultery,' I commented.

Percy whistled. 'You think Nathalie suspects an affair?'

'It's possible. I'm going to watch Nathalie and Rupert tonight and see how they behave towards each other.' I had the dinner party at Smugglers Haunt to look forward to that evening.

'One way or another, Emerald seems to have been involved with Arnold Rowe and Rupert Keats,' Millicent observed.

'How involved, I wonder? She might know more about Arnold's death than she's letting on. She was an actress, after all.' I turned to Percy. 'Perhaps you should get to know her better? Over a brandy. Also, try to find out more about Joyce Rowe.'

'I like the sound of this mission.' Percy stroked his moustache. 'I'll do it when we come back from the pictures.'

'I don't mind not going,' Millicent said quickly. 'If you'd like to spend more time with Emerald.' Percy had talked her into going to the cinema to see the latest Douglas Fairbanks film and she wasn't overly excited at the prospect.

'And miss the movie? It's supposed to be one of his best.' Percy shook his head. 'It will be better to wait until the other guests have gone to bed and Emerald cracks open the contraband.'

'Just don't overdo the brandy,' I warned. 'Emerald could be a dangerous woman.'

Percy shuddered. 'I'm certain she is.'

13

A long dining table had been placed by the panoramic windows and as we ate, we watched the sun set on Smugglers Cove.

Nathalie and Rupert were relaxed hosts, and there was a family atmosphere to the occasion. Emile had prepared a five-course meal, which gave me plenty of time to analyse the other guests.

The couples seated around the table were examples of different generations of marriage. Gramps and Nan were the oldest couple in terms of age and length of married life. They'd been married for over fifty years and were perfectly attuned with each other.

Marc and his wife, Annette, were the youngest married couple. I remembered Marc telling me they were childhood sweethearts. He'd been twenty-four when I'd first met him, so must be thirty now. Annette was a year younger. I wondered how their relationship had evolved from first love into a nearly ten-year marriage. It can't have been easy for them to have left family and friends behind and start again in a new country. Annette seemed unsure of herself and often looked to Marc or Nathalie to explain certain parts of the conversation – her heavily accented English wasn't as fluent as theirs. I wondered how she'd cope in London without Nathalie to turn to. I had a sneaking suspicion that Marc wanted to remove his wife from her friend's influence.

Then there were the soon-to-be weds, my father and Katherine. I had to admit there was a chemistry between them. Their shared glances showed they knew what the other was thinking. Seated next to them were the contentedly married Stephen and Gwen, who seemed completely at ease together.

Rupert and Nathalie were a different matter. They weren't such a comfortable pairing as the other couples. Although they were relaxed hosts, there was a sense of disconnect between them. The only time they appeared to be in harmony was when their son, Timothy, was present. He'd been allowed to stay up to greet the guests, and they'd showed him off proudly before he was whisked off to bed by Mrs Green.

If either Nathalie or Annette were contemplating divorce, my money would be on Nathalie. However, appearances could be deceptive.

My partner for the evening was Emile, and I wasn't complaining. He was witty and flirtatious – even my grandmother wasn't immune to his charm. As well as being pleasing to look at, he was an accomplished chef. The smell of roasting lamb and rosemary coming from the kitchen was mouth-watering.

Hors-d'œuvres were followed by courses of fried fillets of sole, dressed lobster, lamb noisettes and a desert of bavarois au chocolat.

While Rupert acted as host and kept everyone's glasses topped up, Emile darted in and out of the kitchen, bringing trays of dishes to the table and serving each guest himself. He and

Rupert seemed to have put aside their differences for the evening, although the overly polite way they addressed one another hinted at their animosity.

Conversation flowed easily, the only awkward moment arising when Gramps made reference to my travels around Europe the previous year. My father had given my grandparents an edited version of events and I stuck to this story when Nathalie asked me where I'd been. I made it sound more like an extended holiday than a year spent roaming Europe with a man I'd fallen in love with yet hadn't known that well.

'Did Percy and Millicent accompany you?' Marc asked.

'No. Another friend,' I said vaguely, not looking him in the eye. My father hastily interjected to change the subject.

Shortly after, Stephen stood to make the toasts, first welcoming my father and me to the family. Then we raised a glass to Marc and Annette to wish them well for their new life in London.

Emile was entertaining company, describing the dishes he'd prepared and telling stories about the hotel. It was a shame Millicent wasn't with me to enjoy it. She would have lapped it up. Instead, she was watching Douglas Fairbanks running around Sherwood Forest in green stockings as Robin Hood.

After dinner, we sat in the lounge, having drifted into various groups. My father was deep in conversation with Stephen, Gwen chatted with my grandparents, while Nathalie, Emile, Marc and Annette stayed at the dining table, conversing animatedly in Dutch. Rupert and Mrs Green circulated with drinks – I noticed Rupert topped up his own brandy more than once.

I took the opportunity to talk with Katherine. 'How does it feel to be back at Smugglers Haunt?'

She smiled. 'I'll admit, I was a little apprehensive about how

I'd feel. It brings back so many memories. Laurence and I were happy here and I hope Rupert, Nathalie and Timothy are too.' She glanced towards Rupert as she said this, and I saw doubt in her eyes.

'Do you miss it?'

'I miss living by the sea. It was heavenly to wake up to that view each morning and walk down to the cove.'

'Did Superintendent Endicott talk to you?'

She nodded. 'There wasn't much I could tell him. I remember Mr Rowe doing odd jobs here, and Mrs Rowe helping Mrs Green with the cleaning. I've no idea how the poor man ended up in the cave.'

'Were you here on the day they think he went missing?'

She shook her head. 'I don't remember the day. According to my diary, I was in London. I hadn't wanted to go; I was summoned by the war office to help with some admin. Stephen and Gwen always called in while I was away, and it's likely Rupert was here. He knew Laurence wouldn't recover and tried to spend what remaining time he could with his brother.'

If what Stephen suspected was correct, Rupert had taken advantage of his brother's condition to ensure he inherited the villa. At the same time, had he been using the cove to smuggle spirits to sell in his shop?

'And, of course, Mrs Green was here,' Katherine continued. 'It was an awful time. Now knowing how long Laurence had left. I was so glad I was with him when he died.'

I nodded, wondering how to diplomatically ask what work had been so important she'd had to leave her dying husband's bedside.

In December 1918, my father and I had been living in Hither Green. We didn't move back to Walden until later the following year. Although Father had said he wanted us to return to Walden, I'd resisted, only agreeing to the move after he'd arranged for me to work with Elijah at *The Walden Herald*. By that time, I'd failed to get a job with any of the London newspapers, and it had seemed the only option.

In the back of my mind was the niggling suspicion that my father could have been seeing Katherine before the major's death. I was about to ask more about her war work when we were interrupted by Annette asking Rupert if we could go out to the terrace.

'The sea looks beautiful,' she said in her accented English. 'It's so romantic.' She smiled and took Marc's hand.

'Of course.' Rupert opened the terrace door, and we watched him light the oil lamps. It was after ten o'clock, and the combination of flickering lamps and the moonlit sea made a charming scene.

Katherine and I went out to the terrace, followed by my father and grandparents, and Stephen and Gwen. The cove below was in semi-darkness, and I couldn't help but think of the musty cave where Arnold Rowe had lain for so long. I noticed mine weren't the only eyes drawn to the dark shadows at the foot of the cliff. Perhaps old Dick Endicott, in search of his lost treasure, wasn't the only ghost to haunt Smugglers Cove.

Gradually, we began to drift back inside, content to admire the view from the comfort of the sofas. The evening was coming to an end and my grandmother refused Rupert's offer of another drink. 'I'll be falling asleep if I have any more.'

My father knew this was his cue. 'I'd better get you home.'

'I'll fetch your coat,' Rupert said. But he made no move to go. Instead, he stayed where he was and seemed to sway a little. I noticed his brow was covered in sweat.

Nan reached up to pat his arm. 'Are you feeling unwell, my

dear?' This was her polite way of saying that perhaps Rupert had drunk too much.

'Just a...' He never finished the sentence. His body went limp and he slid down the side of my grandmother's armchair, collapsing onto the carpet.

14

'Rupert collapsed?' Millicent stopped brushing her hair and looked at my reflection in the mirror. She'd been asleep when we'd eventually got home the night before, and I'd been so tired, I'd decided the news could wait until morning.

'It was nearly eleven, and Nan thought it was time we were going. Rupert said he'd get her coat. The next minute, he was slumped on the floor.'

'Was he drunk?'

'He had been drinking – wine with dinner and then brandy. I'm not sure how many he had. But he hadn't seemed drunk before then.'

'Poor man.' Millicent stood up and began to make her bed.

'Stephen and Gwen decided it was best to take him to hospital rather than wake the local doctor. He's sleeping it off there.' I took Millicent's place in front of the mirror. 'How was your evening? Did you like the Palladium?'

Exeter boasted three cinemas, and the Palladium was the biggest and the best. During the war, I'd visited it occasionally with my grandparents to watch Charlie Chaplin films. Nan and I had been as entertained by the tip-up seats and the stencilled paintings on the walls as we had by the movies.

'I've never been to such a large cinema. It's so spacious, and the seats were very comfortable,' she enthused.

'And the film?' I suspected she'd liked this less.

'Percy enjoyed it,' she laughed.

'He does love Douglas Fairbanks.'

'He wants to be Douglas Fairbanks even when the silly man is dressed in ridiculous stockings and has a feather in his hat. Tonight, we have *The Second Mrs Tanqueray* to look forward to.'

'How about coming on a boring shopping trip with me as an antidote to all that drama?'

'I already have a dress to wear to the wedding.'

'You can help me choose one.'

She sighed. 'Iris. Katherine wants to spend the day with you. I'm going to the museum.'

I pouted. 'But a whole day shopping?'

'And lunch. You might just enjoy it.'

We went downstairs to find Katherine having breakfast with my father and grandparents. Stephen had dropped her off on his way to work.

'Have you heard how Captain Keats is?' I asked.

'He's quite ill, I'm afraid. He didn't regain consciousness overnight. They're not sure what's wrong with him. Nathalie's still there, and Stephen and I are going to call in on our way home this afternoon.'

'Do you think he ate something that didn't agree with him?' Millicent suggested.

'I'm afraid he was drinking rather a lot,' Nan said. 'I think it's more likely to be that. Emile's food was divine.' She began to describe each dish in detail to Millicent, who sighed with envy.

After breakfast, Millicent, Katherine and I walked into town.

Ignoring my pleading glance, Millicent insisted on parting company with us at Colson's department store, saying she was keen to get to the museum.

Reluctantly, I followed Katherine inside and up the stairs to ladies clothing, where we perused the racks. I had no idea what I was looking for. What did you wear for your father's wedding?

At first, Katherine diplomatically refrained from offering any suggestions, though when she saw I was making no progress, she began to pick a selection of dresses for me to try on.

In the fitting rooms, she waited patiently for me to emerge. I stood awkwardly in front of her while she inspected me. She shook her head over each dress, which was a relief as they were all too fussy for my taste.

She handed the discarded dresses to the shop assistant and told me to wait while she found some more. I hovered uncomfortably in my slip, wondering how long this nightmare would last. To my surprise, she came back with just one dress and handed it to me. It was pale blue silk, cut in a simple style with a dropped waist and pleated skirt.

'Try it on.'

I went back into the changing room and slipped it over my head, enjoying the feel of the cool silk. When I gazed in the full-length mirror, I liked what I saw.

I showed it to Katherine and she smiled. 'It's perfect. Do you want it?'

I nodded. I hadn't even noticed the price tag.

'Good. Now we have the dress, we can look for some shoes and a hat to go with it.'

I protested but she insisted. 'I promised you a new outfit for the wedding.'

I knew I was being bribed and decided to go along with it. Everything became easier after that. We settled on a cream-coloured cloche hat that fitted close to the face and sat low over the eyes and a pair of delicate cream suede shoes. I'd never owned such pretty clothes. I habitually wore trousers, much to the consternation of the staider residents of Walden, and knew my father would be pleased by the feminine outfit.

'Thank you. It's very generous of you.'

'It's my pleasure.' She smiled. 'Let's go to Dellers on Bedford Street for lunch.'

I'd never been to Dellers before and had secretly always wanted to go there. The one on Bedford Street was particularly impressive, built in a baroque style. The grand entrance led into a domed atrium that covered the main café in the basement and the first and second-floor balconies.

Katherine and I sat on the first-floor balcony and enjoyed a luncheon of cold ham and tongue, new potatoes and salad, followed by fruit tart and custard. We chatted easily while listening to Gwen Master and her orchestra playing below.

'Poor Rupert. I do hope he'll be alright.' She said this with concern, but I didn't detect any real affection in her voice.

'He didn't even seem particularly drunk, although he did drink a lot.'

'Rupert has always known how to stay just the right side of drunk.'

'Do you know him well?'

She shook her head. 'I hadn't spent much time with him before Laurence became ill. Our paths had crossed occasionally, mainly at weddings and funerals. Laurence and Rupert's parents died within months of each other. Then, at the start of the war, Rupert came to live in Exeter. He'd been living in Plymouth before that.'

'He began to spend time at Smugglers Haunt?'

'At first, he was away fighting. He'd been honourably

discharged when Laurence was poisoned and shipped home in September of 1918 and visited often after that. He was a great help to me. He would get Laurence's prescriptions from Dr Frampton's surgery.' She smiled. 'Although that may have been because of Nathalie. She was the receptionist there. Rupert was besotted with her.'

'And she liked him too?'

'I'll admit, I was a little surprised when she agreed to marry him. Rupert is a charming man, but there's a twenty-two-year age gap, and Nathalie wasn't short of admirers though Dawlish isn't blessed with many eligible bachelors.'

Why had Nathalie chosen the charming Captain Keats? I suspected she'd opted for financial security and Smugglers Haunt over romance.

'Did you know about the codicil that was added to your husband's will?'

'It came as a complete shock. Stephen was angry and wanted to challenge it.' She shrugged. 'I didn't have the heart. After losing Laurence, I needed to get away from Devon for a while. I had the flat in London, so I thought, why not let Rupert and Nathalie embark on married life with the security of their own home? I hoped it would give Rupert the stability he's lacked since he left the army.'

I got the impression Katherine realised Nathalie wouldn't have taken on Rupert without Smugglers Haunt. 'That was kind of you.'

'Perhaps it was what Laurence had wanted. Rupert is a weak man, but with Nathalie's influence, I thought he'd be able to make a go of things.'

From what I'd heard, Rupert wasn't making much of a go of his wine importing business.

'And Rupert did spend a lot of time with Laurence when he

was dying,' she continued. 'I wanted to stay at home to care for him, but it wasn't always possible. Even after the war ended, there was still so much to do, assisting refugees to locate their relatives in Belgium and return home. Rupert was a great help. He was always happy to close the shop and come and sit with Laurence.'

I wondered what else Rupert got up to when he was at Smugglers Haunt.

'How did you become involved with helping refugees?'

'It started off in a small way. The volunteers at the refugee centres often called on me because I could speak Dutch. After Laurence joined the intelligence corps, he was away a lot, and I began to spend more time at the refugee centres.' She paused. 'Then I was approached by a department within the war office and asked to start taking written testimonies and gathering information.'

'Gathering information?' I sat upright. This was news to me.

'They wanted to know what the refugees could tell them about troop movements in and out of Belgium, which towns and cities were used as army bases, and the activities of local resistance groups. And...' She lowered her voice. 'Civilian executions.'

'Were there many?' I hardly dared ask the question.

'The German army killed thousands of French and Belgian civilians between August and November 1914 in what appeared to be random large-scale attacks. The volunteers at the centre let it be known that anyone with information should contact me.' She sighed. 'Hundreds of refugees wanted to bear witness – tell of the atrocities they'd seen. It was a laborious process and took a while to get coordinated. It wasn't until mid-1915 that we had formal channels to coordinate and communicate all the information.'

'I remember when I was at the Park Fever Hospital, there were Flemish-speaking officials who would interview the new arrivals.'

'That's where you met Emile and Marc?'

I nodded. 'They knew Nathalie and Annette had ended up on a train to Devon. I wrote to Nan, and she was able to track them down quite easily.'

She smiled. 'Clementina practically ran the Southernhay centre. She was a force of nature.'

As we chatted about my grandparents, my thoughts drifted back to what Katherine had told me about her war work. Although it explained why she'd occasionally had to go up to London and leave Major Keats, I still didn't understand why she'd given up Smugglers Haunt so easily. Especially when it must have been obvious that Rupert had behaved unscrupulously to get it. She'd said herself he was besotted with Nathalie and that must have been his motivation.

After lunch, we browsed a few more shops before strolling back to Bedford Circus. We arrived to find Stephen Damerell's car parked outside. Next to it was a Black Maria.

Katherine's face fell when she saw it. 'Something's happened.'

Stephen and Superintendent Endicott were seated with my father and grandparents in the drawing room.

Stephen stood up as we entered. 'I'm afraid I have some bad news. Rupert died earlier today.'

15

'I believe you all dined with Captain and Mrs Keats last night?' Superintendent Endicott said.

'That's right,' my father replied. Katherine sat beside him on the sofa and he took her hand.

Nan and Gramps were sitting in wing-backed armchairs on either side of the fireplace. I perched on the arm of Nan's chair.

'And none of you have suffered any ill effects?' the superintendent asked.

We all shook our heads.

'My wife's fine. And so are Mr and Mrs Jansen.' Stephen stood by the mantelpiece.

'Do you think it was food poisoning?' my father asked.

Superintendent Endicott shrugged. 'We have no idea. It seems strange that no one else was affected.'

'You think it's suspicious then? Could he have been drugged?' I asked.

Superintendent Endicott held up his hand. 'It might be natural causes. A post mortem will tell us more.'

'Because I wondered about Arnold Rowe.' I ignored the exasperated look my father shot in my direction.

The superintendent sighed. 'What about Mr Rowe?'

'Could he have been drugged?' I still thought it odd that he'd been sitting upright and had no injuries.

'It's not something we can tell from the remains. The pathologist's report has been sent to the coroner, who confirmed he has all the information required for an inquest. Mr Rowe has now been buried.'

'Has he? Where?' I was surprised by the speed of this.

'Here in Exeter at the Higher Cemetery at his wife's request.'

Joyce Rowe hadn't wasted any time.

Superintendent Endicott stood up. 'Thank you for your time. Depending on the results of the post mortem, I may need to ask some further questions.'

My grandfather showed him out.

'Poor Rupert. And poor Nathalie and little Timothy,' Katherine said tearfully. My father put his arm around her. It was less than two weeks to the wedding and she was probably wondering what else could go wrong.

Stephen placed his teacup on the table. 'Sad business. I didn't like the man, but I can't see anyone wanting to harm him. Chap's heart probably gave out.'

'I expect you're right.' Gramps had returned and was helping Nan clear up the tea things.

I followed Stephen and Katherine into the hallway where I'd left the shopping bags. Hesitantly, I gave her a hug. 'Thank you for a lovely day and for treating me to such a beautiful outfit. I'm sorry it ended so badly.'

She seemed to brighten a little. 'It was fun, wasn't it? Perhaps we can have some days out together in the future. Just the two of us?'

'I'd like that,' I replied.

After she left, I was rewarded with a hug from my father and a small glass of Nan's sherry. I enjoyed both.

* * *

That evening, Millicent and I got dressed up for the theatre. Nan had said we should invite Percy in, but knowing that Emerald was with him, we dashed out to the car as soon as we heard the toot of the horn.

Emerald sat in the front seat, looking dazzling in a turquoise dress with a matching turban. Her nails and lips were painted crimson, and around her neck was a long string of green beads. The cloying scent of her orange blossom perfume filled the car and I had to open the window.

Percy drove us to the Theatre Royal on Longbrook Street. While Millicent and I climbed out of the back of the car, Emerald stayed in the front passenger seat, waiting for Percy to jump out and come around to open the door for her.

Millicent and I watched in amusement as she stepped out like royalty. The doorman came forward to greet her with a bow.

'Miss Dubois, a pleasure to see you.'

Emerald inclined her head graciously. This performance continued as we entered the theatre, where she was welcomed by the box office attendant and various ushers.

'I'm going backstage to see Dame Cicely and Mr Andrews. Be a darling and get me a large gin,' she called to Percy, twirling her string of green beads.

He gave a theatrical bow and we followed him into the bar. Millicent and I perched on cushioned stools while Percy went to get the drinks. He returned with two sherries, a large gin and a whisky and soda.

'Did you and Emerald have a cosy chat last night?' I asked.

He leant forward and whispered, 'It appears she and the captain may have taken comfort in each other's arms.'

'An affair?'

'Not as such. She made it sound more like an unfortunate encounter. He was drowning his sorrows and they got friendly. According to Emerald, he's obsessed with Nathalie. However, his wife isn't as keen on him. His business is going badly and Nathalie had higher expectations of her husband.'

'What about Joyce Rowe? Did you find out anything about her?' Millicent asked.

'Only what we already know. She and Arnold did not get along. The marriage was a disaster from the start, and it seems there were rumours about her taking up with Fred Pike, the ironmonger, when Arnold was away during the war. From the sound of it, Arnold was no angel in that respect either.'

'So Joyce wouldn't have welcomed his return,' I commented. 'She may have decided to get rid of her unwanted husband.'

'Emerald has her suspicions, although they don't appear to be based on any actual evidence. There's no love lost between the two women.'

'Has she heard about Captain Keats' death?' Millicent asked.

'Oh yes, everyone in Dawlish is talking about it. News around here travels fast.'

'She doesn't seem too distraught.'

'She was prostrate with grief for a whole minute.' He sipped his whisky and soda. 'What did Endicott say? Does he think the death is suspicious?'

'He's not sure. There's to be a post mortem,' I replied.

'People are saying it was his heart,' Percy said. 'Could it have been a heart attack?'

I shrugged. 'He looked a bit pale and sweaty, then sort of

slumped down. It could have been his heart, I suppose. We all thought he'd had a bit too much to drink.'

'Did he utter any last words? Accuse anyone of doing him in?'

'He told my grandmother he'd go and fetch her coat.'

'Hmm, I'm not sure your grandmother sounds a likely suspect.'

'A suspect?' Emerald sank onto the stool next to him and took a swig of gin. 'Who's a suspect? Did someone kill poor old Rupert?'

I explained about our visit from Superintendent Endicott. 'He also told us that Arnold Rowe has been buried here in Exeter in the Higher Cemetery.'

'Already?' Emerald swung her green beads. 'With no funeral? That woman's got a nerve.'

I guessed she was referring to Joyce Rowe.

'It's a shame there was no funeral. I would have liked to have gone,' Millicent said.

'It's a disgrace. Bet she couldn't wait to get him six feet under so she can tie the knot with Fred Pike. Well, I'm going to visit his grave and pay my respects whether she likes it or not.'

Millicent nodded. 'I think we should visit the cemetery, too.'

Before I could reply, the bell rang. We hastily finished our drinks and made our way into the stalls.

Contrary to my expectations, *The Second Mrs Tanqueray* was an entertaining and thought-provoking drama. It was a little melodramatic at times, but surprisingly well acted by the whole cast, including Dame Cicely and Mr Andrews. Although they weren't on stage for long, they played their parts with aplomb.

* * *

The following afternoon Millicent and I met Percy at Exeter St David's railway station, and the three of us walked to the Higher Cemetery.

Percy seemed a little worse for wear and revealed that when he and Emerald had returned to the Jewel of the Sea, she'd decided to open a bottle of the good brandy in Rupert Keats' honour.

'I vaguely remember drinking to the captain's good health at two o'clock this morning.'

'His good health? The man's dead,' I said.

'Things were rather confused by that time. Mr Andrews and Dame Cicely seemed to think Rupert was a poodle Emerald had once owned.'

Our walk took us along Ladysmith Road, and I pointed out Ladysmith School, where my grandfather had taught for over forty years and where my father had first met Stephen Damerell.

We walked on to the cemetery and stopped by the memorial for the victims of the Great War. A granite cross sat on a tiered base with bronze plaques surrounding the plinth. The inscription read:

In memory of the men who died in this city from the effects of their services overseas in the Great War 1914 – 1918.

It was followed by a long list of names.

'Look at all these graves.' Millicent gazed at the rows of single granite stones inscribed simply with an initial and surname.

'Two hundred and twenty-four in all,' said a gruff voice. We turned to find an old man watching us. He leant on a handcart that contained gardening tools and brushes. 'Civilians and soldiers that died here and overseas.'

'So many?' Millicent murmured.

'It's because of all the military hospitals in the city,' the man explained.

Percy hadn't moved for some time. His cheeks were wet with tears and he was staring unseeingly at the list of names on the plaque.

I indicated to Millicent that we should leave Percy to his silent reverie. She nodded. The man trailed behind us, pushing his handcart. He was about sixty and walked with a limp.

'He'll be remembering his fallen comrades. I see it all the time,' he said quietly. 'Brings it all back. Best give him some time with his thoughts.'

'Perhaps you could help us find a new grave,' Millicent said. 'It's a man called Arnold Rowe whose remains were found in Dawlish recently.'

'I know who you mean. I'll show you.'

We followed him into a new section of the cemetery. I noticed that just like the plot given over to casualties of war, the grass verges were neatly cut and the graves tended with reverence. 'Are you the groundsman here? You've made it look so beautiful.'

'It's a privilege,' he replied.

He took us to where a simple wooden cross etched with the words *Arnold Rowe* marked a grave of freshly dug earth. Someone had already left flowers – pink roses striped with fuchsia, magenta and white.

'What unusual flowers.' Millicent bent down to sniff them. 'They smell divine. I've never seen roses like this before. They're more likely to be from Emerald than Mrs Rowe.'

I knelt down beside her to breathe in the rich, fruity fragrance. The bouquet had been placed loosely in a simple glass jar. 'I think they come from the garden at Smugglers Haunt. Nathalie showed them to me. They're a new variety from France. Did you see who left these?' I asked the groundsman.

'I saw a dark-haired lady by the grave. She was upset,' he replied. 'Here comes your friend. I'll leave you to grieve in peace.' The man nodded at the grave and walked away.

'Is this Arnold's final resting place? Better than that cave. It's quite lovely here. So peaceful.' Percy's attempt to appear his usual cheery self nearly succeeded but for the red eyes and slight hoarseness to his voice. He peered at the flowers. 'Has Emerald been already?'

I shook my head. 'I think Mrs Green brought them.'

'So Mrs Green has left flowers for her nephew, yet it doesn't appear that Joyce Rowe has visited,' Millicent observed. 'Yet Joyce was the one who insisted on his burial here without a funeral.'

I was about to reply when someone called my name. I turned to see Marc Jansen striding towards us.

'Iris, your grandparents told me you were here.' He stopped. 'Is this where Arnold Rowe is buried?'

I nodded. 'We came to pay our respects. What are you doing here?'

Marc cleared his throat. 'I had a visit from Superintendent Endicott this afternoon. The post mortem showed Rupert Keats was poisoned.'

16

'Poisoned?' I repeated. 'With what?'

'Chloral hydrate. It's an anaesthetic. Mixed with alcohol, it can have fatal consequences, as in this case,' Marc explained.

'Gosh,' Millicent said. 'How horrible.'

'Superintendent Endicott wants to interview everyone at the dinner party,' Marc continued. 'He seems to think someone must have put something in Rupert's food or drink.'

'He thinks it was administered at the party? Not before?'

'They can't be sure, but it seems likely,' Marc said. 'Apparently, it would have taken effect pretty quickly, so it must have been that evening.'

'When does Superintendent Endicott want to speak to us?' We began to walk towards the gate of the cemetery, Millicent and Percy following.

'Tomorrow. We've arranged for him to come to the Damerell & Tate offices. It will be less conspicuous than him turning up at all our homes. Stephen and I have cleared our morning appointments so one of us can be with you when you're interviewed.'

'Do you think we need a solicitor?' I said in alarm.

'Probably not,' Marc replied with a smile. 'But if you have an office full of them, you might as well make use of their services.'

I nodded. 'You're right, of course.'

'Stephen's going to drive Katherine and Gwen into town in the morning. I'll bring Annette with me and speak to Emile. It's going to be quite a crowd. But the sooner we get this over with, the better.'

'I'm worried about Emile,' I said softly. The drinks had all been poured by either Rupert or Mrs Green as far as I could remember. But the food had been prepared and served by Emile. Superintendent Endicott was likely to ask him a lot of questions, and Marc and I both knew Emile didn't always keep his patience in situations like this.

'Me too,' he replied. 'I'll brief him before the interview and make sure he keeps his temper under control.'

Marc went back to his office, and Millicent and I walked down Bonhay Road to the railway station with Percy, whose melancholy of earlier seemed to have returned.

'Why don't you come back with us to my grandparents?' I suggested. 'They won't mind you joining us for an early dinner.'

'We could always go to the pictures afterwards,' Millicent said.

I wanted to hug her, knowing how much she would detest another evening at the cinema. But more than that, I wanted to wrap my arms around Percy, who was struggling to hide his sorrow.

'Good grief, woman, you've worn me out with your gallivanting,' Percy joked. 'I'm going back to enjoy a quiet evening in with Emerald's bunch of eccentrics. It's been an odd sort of afternoon, hasn't it?' He stuck his hands in his pockets and ambled away.

'Do you think he'll be alright?' Millicent asked.

I linked my arm through hers. 'He just needs some time alone.'

'Does he ever talk about the war?'

'He once told me that he'd lost some great pals. And that he felt it was his duty to live his life for them, which meant boozing and dancing with as many pretty girls as will have him.'

She smiled. 'That sounds like Percy.'

* * *

Damerell & Tate Solicitors was based on Southernhay West. It was a road I was familiar with from my time volunteering with Nan at the refugee centre.

The offices took up the whole of a three-storey red-brick terrace building. We were greeted by an efficient woman called Miss Briars, who explained that the interviews would take place in Stephens's office, and she'd moved some chairs into a spare room where we could wait our turn.

She ushered my father, my grandparents and me into an office, where we found Gwen, Katherine, Annette and Emile. The only ones who'd been at the dinner party who weren't present were Nathalie Keats and Mrs Green. Marc explained that Superintendent Endicott had interviewed them the day before when he'd informed them Rupert had been poisoned.

Despite the circumstances, we were a cheery bunch. It was apparent that no one had cared too much for Rupert Keats. There was shock and some sadness over his death, but not grief. Annette and Gwen talked about little Timothy and how best to help Nathalie. My grandparents discussed wedding arrangements with my father and Katherine while Emile kept me entertained with tales from the kitchens at the Royal Clarence Hotel.

I suspected the person enjoying themselves the least was Superintendent Endicott. I wasn't privy to the other interviews, but I was pretty sure he'd listened to nearly a dozen identical accounts of the same dinner party. Apart from Rupert collapsing, nothing of interest had happened that evening. We'd chatted and eaten delicious food.

When it was my turn, Marc escorted me to Stephen's office.

Superintendent Endicott sat behind a large desk. 'You seem to be having a lively holiday, Miss Woodmore.' He didn't smile. 'You discovered the remains of Mr Rowe, and you were present when Captain Keats was drugged.'

I wondered if I was a suspect. 'Do you think there's a connection between the two deaths? They knew each other.' I decided not to mention the smuggling as the Superintendent would wonder where I'd got the information from and I didn't want to incriminate Emerald or Owen.

'That's something my investigation will look into. Shall we concentrate on the events that led to Captain Keats' death?' Superintendent Endicott replied dryly. 'You're clearly an observant young lady. Is there anything you can tell us about the dinner party?'

I guessed what was of most interest to him was our account of how the food and drinks had been served. 'Emile Vandamme was the chef, and he and Mrs Green brought in each course on platters. The serving was rather random. I don't think it would have been possible to be certain which portion of food ended up on Rupert Keats' plate.'

'You don't think it could have been contrived?' He didn't sound convinced.

'No, I don't.'

However, I wasn't certain. If Emile had planned it in advance, perhaps he could have made sure which portion he gave to Rupert.

'What about the drinks?'

'Captain Keats poured the wine at dinner and the spirits afterwards. Mrs Green came in with a tray of tea and coffee, and she poured those. She may have served some of the other drinks, I didn't notice.' I thought back to the wines and spirits that had been offered. They'd all come straight from the decanters, so it would be difficult to know where the drug would end up. 'How is chloral hydrate usually administered?'

'Orally, as a sleeping draught. Criminals have been known to use it to render their victims unconscious in order to rob them. I've also heard of unscrupulous boxing promoters using it to rig fights. A few drops can make a boxer drowsy.'

'Yes, Captain Keats did look sleepy. How long before it takes effect?'

'Miss Woodmore, so far, you've asked me more questions than I've asked you.'

'Sorry,' I said, then added, 'Where would you obtain chloral hydrate?'

I saw Marc suppress a grin. My interview with Superintendent Endicott came to an end shortly after that.

17

The following day, Millicent, Percy and I received an invitation from Horace Laffaye to dine with him and Elijah at the Royal Clarence Hotel. We eagerly accepted. No doubt news of Captain Keats' sudden death had reached their ears, and they wanted to hear the latest gossip.

Once an assembly rooms, in the eighteenth century, the Royal Clarence had become the first establishment in the country to be described as a hotel. Its columned entrance looked across to Exeter Cathedral.

Millicent and I put on our second-best frocks. I'd have to save the pale blue one for the wedding. Millicent was keeping her best dress in its cover until the big day. She hadn't even shown it to me yet.

Horace and Elijah were seated in the lounge with whisky and sodas in front of them. I told them about my interview with the police.

'Endicott has my sympathies.' Elijah laughed. 'I'm sure he and Superintendent Cobbe would enjoy comparing notes.'

Percy arrived wearing his new blue flannel trousers. He

seemed to have done something odd to his moustache. When I asked what it was, he scowled at me.

'It's wax. Mr Andrews lent me some of his special concoction. Emerald thinks it looks splendid.' He took a swig of whisky and soda as soon as the waiter placed it in front of him.

'Emerald?' Horace enquired. 'And Mr Andrews?'

'Miss Emerald Dubois is the landlady of the Jewel of the Sea guest house where I'm staying in Dawlish,' Percy explained.

'Real name Elsie Dobson,' I added before reaching for my sherry.

Elijah gave a snort of laughter.

'Emerald's her stage name – she gave it up because... Oh, never mind all that. Many of her guests are theatrical types. Mr Andrews is currently starring in *The Second Mrs Tanqueray* at the Theatre Royal, along with another of the guests, Dame Cicely Campbell.'

'Not a real dame.' I thought 'starring in' was exaggerating Dame Cicely and Mr Andrews' few minutes on stage.

'The Jewel of the Sea sounds a most interesting establishment,' Horace commented.

'It's a hoot. We're having a beach party on Saturday. You should come along; I'll introduce you to Emerald and her guests. We've hired some beach huts and we're going swimming in Coryton Cove. It used to be called the Gentlemens' Bathing Cove when the beach was segregated. The ladies' beach was near the Blenheim Hotel, and they used to have those old-fashioned bathing machines that you can wheel into the sea so ladies can bathe privately. There's still one at Coryton Cove that's in use.'

Horace clapped his hands together. 'I haven't seen one of those in years. I always thought it was the most decorous way to bathe.' He turned to Elijah. 'Wouldn't it be refreshing to go into the sea?'

Elijah grunted.

'And, of course, she has a well-stocked cellar. Well, cave, to be precise.' Percy regaled them with the tale of the smugglers' cave at the back of the boarding house.

Elijah brightened at this. 'I suppose it might be pleasant to sit on the beach.'

'I should like to see this cave,' Horace added.

We finished our drinks and followed our noses through to the restaurant. Waiters flitted between tables carrying silver salvers, and we drooled at the sight and smell of venison, dauphine potatoes and French asparagus in melted butter.

'Should we be worried that the chef here might be a poisoner?' Percy said cheerfully as we walked across the marble-floored dining room.

'Shut up,' I hissed. 'Don't spread malicious rumours.'

'That's a rotten thing to say. Emile couldn't possibly have done it,' Millicent whispered.

We refrained from discussing the murders while we perused the menu and the waiter took our orders. Horace was in good spirits and insisted on treating us to caviar appetisers and champagne. Finger bowls filled with rose-scented water were positioned between the array of silver cutlery and crystal glasses that covered the pristine white tablecloth.

'Could Emile have tampered with the food?' Percy asked when the waiter was out of earshot. 'You said he served it. He could have put something in Rupert's portion.'

I shook my head. 'It would have been too risky. If he had poisoned the food, it could have ended up on anyone's plate. Emile would never do that.'

Percy pouted. 'You just don't want it to be him.'

Elijah raised an eyebrow.

Millicent intervened, ever the peacemaker. 'Why would he do

it at a dinner party where he was preparing the food? He'd know the police would question him.'

I gave her a grateful smile. 'He went out of his way to make it a special meal to celebrate the wedding and Marc and Annette's new start in London. It's more likely the drug was slipped into his drink. After dinner there was more movement, everyone was mingling.'

'If not Emile, who?' Percy sipped his champagne and dove into the caviar appetisers.

'No one seems to have disliked Captain Keats,' Millicent observed. 'Yet no one seems to be overly upset by his death.'

'Suspicion might fall on Nathalie,' I said. 'I think she'd tired of the marriage.'

'Getting tired of your marriage isn't generally a cause for murder,' Elijah commented.

'Millicent is right. Rupert Keats doesn't seem to have aroused strong feelings one way or the other. Nathalie didn't give me the impression she hated her husband. But I don't think she was in love with him any more, if she ever had been.' I savoured my last mouthful of caviar. I needed to leave room for my sirloin of beef.

'Far too old for her,' Percy said between mouthfuls.

'She's bound to be a suspect,' Millicent said. 'They say poison is a woman's weapon of choice. Especially if it's a man she wants to murder. No strength is needed.'

'Can it be a coincidence that we uncover a body at Smugglers Haunt and then shortly afterwards Rupert Keats is dead?' I asked.

'He didn't own Smugglers Haunt at the time of Arnold Rowe's death,' Millicent pointed out.

'Katherine lived there at the time and she had no cause to like Rupert Keats. He took Smugglers Haunt from her.' I felt disloyal saying it, but we had to consider every possibility.

Elijah protested. 'Do you seriously see her lacing his food or drink with chloral hydrate?'

'She bought you a lovely dress.' Millicent dabbed delicately at the corners of her mouth with the heavy linen napkin.

'What's that got to do with it?' I said, exasperated. 'I don't really think she's a murderer, but she is marrying my father, so I ought to consider the possibility.'

Elijah grunted and Horace chuckled.

Conversation moved on to talk of the beach party as the waiters cleared the table and fresh dishes arrived. Horace and Elijah were reassured that they could always adjourn to the nearby Blenheim Hotel if it became too hot – or the guests a little too boisterous.

Once we were tucking into our main courses, talk turned once again to the topic of murder.

'What about Mrs Green?' Millicent suggested between mouthfuls of poached salmon in lobster sauce. 'Say Captain Keats and Arnold Rowe argued – over the smuggling operation or the fraudulent witnessing of the will. Captain Keats ends up killing Arnold Rowe and putting his body in the cave. Mrs Green may have known about the smuggling. As we've said, it would be hard to keep it hidden from someone in the house. When the body is found, she realises that Captain Keats must have killed her nephew.'

Horace nodded. 'That's the most sensible suggestion I've heard so far.'

Millicent looked pleased.

Elijah didn't seem convinced. 'Murder for some tax-free tobacco and spirits?'

'Murder for money and Smugglers Haunt,' I corrected. 'Rupert needed cash, and getting duty-free booze and selling it at full price through his shop could have been the difference between him staying solvent or going under. And potentially having to sell Smugglers Haunt, the house he claims was supposed to stay in the male line of the family.'

Horace paused in devouring a dish of quails souvaroff to comment. 'If Arnold Rowe was his only hope of bringing in smuggled goods, why kill him?'

'Arnold could have threatened to reveal the truth about Major Keats' will...'

Percy was about to say something, but I held up my hand to stop him.

'It's Emile,' I whispered.

Emile had emerged from the kitchen in his chef's whites. He came over to our table and made a great show of kissing me on the cheek and taking Millicent's hand.

I introduced him to Horace and Elijah.

'Your food is exceptional, Mr Vandamme.'

'Thank you, Mr Laffaye, I'm so pleased you have enjoyed it.' Emile turned to Percy. 'Percee, there is dancing here tonight. You love dancing, do you not? I will join you in the ballroom later. I cannot let you have these two ladies all to yourself.'

Percy demurred. 'The style of dancing here might be too formal for my taste.'

This was true. Percy's dancing could be a little exuberant for the Royal Clarence Hotel. It was more suited to the basement of the Foxtrot Club in Soho.

Emile turned his attention to Millicent. 'Would you do the honour of dancing with me?'

'Oh well, yes, of course.' Millicent seemed flustered, torn between loyalty to Percy and a desire to please Emile.

Emile kissed her hand. 'I will see you later,' he said with a wink.

I regarded her blushes with amusement. Percy was less pleased.

'We hadn't planned on staying for dances,' he said accusingly.

'I could hardly refuse, could I?' Millicent fanned her face with her napkin.

'Make sure he doesn't slip something in your drink.'

I wasn't sure if he was being serious or not.

After dinner, we adjourned to the ballroom where Horace and Elijah sat, brandies in hand, tapping along to the music.

The Royal Clarence wasn't as staid as expected, and once I got Percy onto the dance floor, he couldn't help but join in. He did love to dance and we hopped around more energetically than any of the other couples. Millicent looked perfectly satisfied to be twirled around at a more sedate pace by Emile.

We swapped partners for the next dance, and I found myself in Emile's arms, which I enjoyed at much as Millicent had.

'How is Nathalie?' I asked.

'She is sad, and so is little Timmy. I've been spending lots of time with him. I think it will be best for them to leave Smugglers Haunt and come with me to London.'

'You're going too?' I couldn't hide my surprise.

'It's time to move on. I have to find a new place to live anyway. Dr Frampton wants to retire and sell the surgery and move to a bungalow. I've been asking around, and I'm sure I can get a job in one of the big hotels. It will be a step up. I love Devon. And the Framptons. But to be in the capital city...' He gave a wolfish grin, showing even white teeth.

'Are you sure Nathalie will want to move?' I asked doubtfully.

'Oh yes. We've often talked of it. She thinks there will be more opportunities there for Timmy as he grows up.'

I felt discomfited by his words. Nathalie had said how much she'd miss Annette. Yet it appeared she and Emile had been planning to go too. With Rupert out of the way, she was free to do what she wanted.

18

'When did my father meet Katherine?' I sank heavily into the cushioned chair, feeling the combined effects of rich food, too much wine and lively dancing.

'I believe they were acquainted as children.' Elijah was watching Horace and Millicent gliding sedately across the dance floor.

Emile was dancing with a very pretty young lady while Percy seemed to have been landed with the girl's mother.

'You know what I mean.' I narrowed my eyes at his prevarication. 'I get the impression neither you nor my father are being entirely truthful with me. When did they start seeing each other?'

'I don't know.'

'The first I knew of Katherine's existence was when I visited the apartment in Paris where they were staying at the end of 1921.'

'Iris. I can't give you the answers you're looking for because I don't know.' He paused. 'If it matters that much to you, speak to your father. Or you could just leave things alone and be happy for them.'

Why couldn't I leave it alone? Was I wrong to be suspicious of my future stepmother? A man's body had been discovered at Smugglers Cove and he'd obviously been killed there during the time Katherine was living in the villa. Her husband appeared to be recovering and then he'd suddenly died. And now Captain Keats had been poisoned, a man who, according to Stephen Damerell, swindled Katherine out of her home.

I was about to put these points to Elijah, when he asked, 'When did you first meet Emile?'

'In June 1917, when I was volunteering at the Park Fever Hospital.' I explained that Emile and Marc had been searching for Nathalie and Annette and my grandmother had helped to locate them.

'How old were you then?'

'I'd just turned eighteen.'

'Did you mention Emile to your father?'

'Why would I?'

'He's a handsome young man. Did you have a romance?' he asked. 'He certainly seems to remember you fondly.'

'No, we didn't. Emile and Marc were among hundreds of refugees who stayed at the hospital during the war. Why would I mention them to my father? He was probably away at the time.'

'Your father also came into contact with many people during the war. Why do you think he should have mentioned them all to you?'

'Not all – just any he became romantically involved with.'

'He didn't become involved with anyone.'

'You just said you didn't know when their romance started.'

'Does it matter?' He sighed and turned his attention back to the dancing. 'This is the problem with holidays.'

'What is?'

'Too much time on your hands. Why don't you go and visit some stately homes or go for bracing walks along the coast? If you're really missing work, you can come up with some new ideas for the August editions of *The Walden Herald*. It's always a quiet time of year. Otherwise, you'll spend the whole month hanging around the magistrate's court, hoping someone decides to do something more illegal than poaching.'

This gave me an idea. It might be worth visiting the local newspaper office to see if I could view old editions, specifically around December 1918.

Before I could reply, Emile appeared by my side and took my hand. 'I claim the last dance.'

I smiled and joined him on the dance floor for a slow waltz.

His eyes twinkled. 'I think I make Percee jealous.'

'Percy's a bit protective of Millicent and me.'

'Hmm. I think it is a little more than that.'

'We're just friends.'

He glanced at Percy and gave a wicked grin. 'In that case, once I'm settled in London, perhaps you'll come and see me? I would like to go back to the place where we first met. That stately old hospital with its ornate water tower. Do you ever go there?'

I smiled. 'I used to be able to see the water tower from my bedroom window when we lived on Hither Green Lane. My father and I moved away, but I still go back to Hither Green to see my gran and aunt. They live just around the corner from the hospital.'

'We will go and visit the old place and then I will take you dancing in a fancy hotel.'

I prevaricated. 'I'm sure you'll find plenty of women to dance with in London.'

'But I want to dance with you,' he whispered. 'Don't you want to dance with me?'

I enjoyed the feeling of his hot breath on my neck. The smell of his spicy cologne was quite intoxicating. Or it could have been the wine. The fragrance had a heat that matched Emile's personality.

'Perhaps we could...' I stopped. Out of the corner of my eye, I saw a man watching us from the side of the dance floor. Unlike the other guests, he wasn't in evening dress. He wore a raincoat over a plain suit.

'Perhaps we could what?' Emile whispered. 'I won't take no for an answer.'

'Emile, I have a bad feeling.'

His eyes followed mine. 'Why? What is it? Do you know that man?'

I shook my head. 'I think he may be a policeman.'

'So what?' He glanced at the man again and his eyes widened. 'You don't think...? Rupert?'

'Emile,' I said urgently. 'If he is here to question you. You will stay calm, won't you?'

His hold on me tightened. 'I didn't do it. You know that, don't you?'

I nodded uncertainly.

Emile didn't release his grip as we moved more awkwardly across the floor.

'I didn't like Rupert, I admit it,' he said. 'But I would never have hurt him. Well, I might have punched him in a temper, but poison? No. He was Timmy's papa. And Nathalie's husband.'

The waltz came to an end, and we took our time leaving the dance floor, staying to clap the orchestra. When Emile led me from the floor, he chose the route furthest away from the man.

We'd nearly reached the table where Horace, Elijah, Percy and Millicent were sitting when our path was blocked.

'Mr Emile Vandamme?'

Emile nodded.

'I'm Sergeant Hoxton of the Devonshire constabulary. I'd

appreciate it if you would accompany me to Exeter police station. I have some questions I'd like to ask you.'

'How dare you come to my place of work at this time of night,' Emile growled. 'If you would like to ask me questions, I will visit you at a civilised time tomorrow morning.'

'You will come with me now, sir,' the sergeant insisted.

'I will not.'

'I think, Mr Vandamme, it would be prudent to do as the sergeant asks.' Horace's tone was both reassuring and resolute. 'I'm sure we can find you some legal representation.'

Emile seemed to realise the wisdom of these words and nodded politely. He turned to me. 'I want Marc. He lives in the basement flat at 15 Bedford Street. Will you go and get him?'

I nodded. 'Stay calm and cooperate. I'll go and see him now.'

'Thank you.' Emile leant forward and kissed my cheek. He smiled graciously at Horace, Elijah, Percy and Millicent, thanked them for the pleasure of their company, then followed the sergeant out of the ballroom.

We watched him go, then stood to leave, trying to exit in a dignified manner, with all eyes upon us. Rather than being embarrassed, Horace seemed highly entertained by the incident.

'Do you know where Bedford Street is?' Elijah took out his cigarettes as soon as we were on the pavement outside.

I nodded. 'It's near to where my grandparents live. We can easily call in on our way back.'

'Don't worry, I'll go too,' Percy assured him. 'And walk with them back to Mr and Mrs Woodmore's house.'

'Good,' Elijah grunted. 'I need my bed.'

We thanked Horace for dinner and he and Elijah began to stroll back to the Rougemont Hotel.

'See you at the beach party on Saturday,' Percy called after them.

They didn't turn, but Horace raised a hand in acknowledgement.

We wandered in the direction of Bedford Street, enjoying the cool evening air after the heat of the ballroom.

Millicent was angry on Emile's behalf. 'Why did that policeman have to come to the hotel like that? Emile might lose his job.'

Even Percy agreed. 'Not a nice thing to do to a chap when he's dancing. Poor show.'

We reached Bedford Street and found number fifteen. Millicent and Percy waited on the pavement while I went down the six steps to the door of the basement flat.

Marc opened the door wearing a sweater and slacks that looked like they'd been pulled on in a hurry. I suddenly realised it was nearly midnight. Briefly, I told him what had happened at the hotel.

'What is it, Marc?' Annette appeared behind him, wearing a pink dressing gown.

'It's Emile. The police have taken him in for questioning about Rupert's death.'

She cupped her hands over her mouth. 'No. Not Emile.' She began to tremble.

Marc put his arm around her. 'Don't worry. I'll go to the police station now. I want to be there when they question him.' He turned back to me. 'Do you want to come in?'

I shook my head, glancing up at Percy and Millicent. 'My friends are waiting, and we should be getting back to my grandparents.'

'Of course. Thank you for coming to tell me. I'll make sure Emile is looked after.' He went to close the door, but Annette was in the way. She seemed frozen in shock. He gently guided her back into the house, kicking the front door closed with his foot.

I wondered if I should have offered to stay with Annette. Marc had a lot to cope with, taking care of her and Emile. I re-joined Millicent and Percy, who'd been watching from the pavement above.

'She seems a nervy sort,' Percy observed.

I explained how she'd lost all her family in Belgium. 'Marc, Nathalie and Emile are all she has.'

'That's probably why she thought you'd be pleased to gain a new mama,' Percy said pointedly.

I scowled, though I recognised the truth of his words. I should be more grateful for the family I had. And was about to gain.

'How sad. No wonder she's frightened. If Emile is tried for murder...' Millicent left the sentence unfinished.

If Emile were found guilty, he'd be sentenced to hang.

19

Millicent and I were woken by the sound of my grandmother's scream.

Wearily, I stumbled out of bed and went downstairs to explain why Percy had slept on the sofa.

By the time we'd left Marc's house the previous night, and Percy had walked us back to Bedford Circus, he'd missed the last train to Dawlish. I'd considered waking my father and asking him to drive Percy to the Jewel of the Sea, but by the time we'd drunk cocoa in the parlour, Percy had fallen asleep. Millicent and I had lifted his legs, so he was lying full length on the sofa, covered him with a blanket and left him snoring.

Nan soon recovered, and while my father lent Percy some toiletries and shaving kit, she began to fry bacon and eggs. Breakfast was a lively affair as we recounted the events of the previous night.

'I'm sure that nice young man had nothing to do with it. Such a good chef,' Nan said as she ladled scrambled eggs onto Percy's plate.

Gramps agreed. 'It's unlikely he'd put poison in the food he was preparing. A chef wouldn't do that.'

I didn't comment. Although I didn't think Emile would have planned to do it, he did sometimes act impulsively.

After breakfast, Father asked Percy if he wanted a ride back to Dawlish. 'I'm going to drive over to see Katherine. I hope this won't upset her too much.'

Percy thanked him but said he'd catch a train later. 'A morning browsing plant specimens in the museum will be calming after the night's events.'

Millicent and I left Percy chatting to my grandparents about his work at the Natural History Museum and got ready to go out. By the time we came back downstairs, Nan was practically flirting with Percy.

'Call me Clementina, my dear. You're welcome to stay here any time,' she said when Percy thanked her and Gramps for their hospitality.

I was about to follow Percy and Millicent out of the front door when Nan took my arm. 'He's a very charming young man,' she whispered.

'You said that about Emile,' I retorted. 'And he's probably just spent the night in a prison cell.'

'Oh, shush.' She slapped me playfully. 'Emile is a lovely young man too, but I've switched my allegiance to Percy.'

I kissed her cheek and caught up with Millicent and Percy outside.

'I'd like to go to Damerell & Tate's to see if there's any news on Emile. Their office is on the next road. It won't take long, and from there we can go on to the museum.'

We walked out of Bedford Circus and along to Southernhay West. Marc emerged as we reached the black front door of the offices.

'Iris. I was coming to find you.'

'What is it?' I asked in alarm. 'How's Emile? Why did they want to question him? Have they released him?'

He held up his hand at the barrage of questions. 'They've still got Emile in custody. The reason they took him in for questioning is because Harriet Green, the housekeeper at Smugglers Haunt, said she overheard Emile threatening Rupert.'

Percy whistled. 'That's not good.'

'It may not be true,' Millicent protested.

Marc was staring at me intently. 'According to Mrs Green, you overheard the threat.'

Millicent and Percy turned to me in surprise.

'Did you? Percy demanded.

I flushed. 'Ah, well, I... I may have done. I wouldn't have called it a threat precisely.'

'What were his exact words?' Marc asked.

'I think he said "you'll be sorry" or something like that. You know what Emile's like. He's probably threatened half of his kitchen staff by now. He didn't mean it.'

'How can you know what he meant?' Percy objected. 'It sounds like he had the means and the motive.'

Marc shot him a look. 'Emile did not poison Rupert.'

'What was their argument about?' Millicent asked. I'd expected her to defend Emile but she appeared thoughtful.

'It was over some wine Rupert had supplied to the hotel. It wasn't the vintage it was supposed to be. Oh yes, that was it: Emile said, "If this costs me my job, you'll regret it."'

'Emile clearly didn't lose his job over it. And would he really murder Captain Keats over some wine?' Millicent seemed more satisfied in Emile's innocence.

'Where were you when you heard the conversation?' Marc asked.

'Er, hiding in some bushes alongside the driveway of Smugglers Haunt,' I admitted.

'She does that sort of thing,' Percy informed him.

Marc sighed and rubbed his chin. 'Superintendent Endicott wants to interview you. You'll have to explain why you were there.'

I groaned. 'I was walking up the driveway of Smugglers Haunt when I heard a car starting up. I moved off the driveway in case it came around the bend at speed. Then I heard raised voices and stayed in the bushes when I realised Emile and Rupert were having a row. I didn't want to embarrass them.' I was pleased with this explanation.

Percy wasn't fooled. 'You wanted to listen in.'

Millicent smiled.

'Can you come with me to the police station?' Marc asked. 'Let's get this over with.'

'What? Now?'

He nodded. 'I want to get Emile out as soon as I can. He needs to get back to work, or he will lose his job. I was going to call on you at your grandparents. We can go there now if you'd like your father to accompany you.'

I shook my head. 'He's gone over to see Katherine. I'm happy to go without him.' I didn't want to admit to my father that I'd been lurking in the bushes at Smugglers Haunt. I'd gone there to see Nathalie to find out what she knew about Katherine.

'Millicent and I will come along as chaperones,' Percy said. 'It sounds more fun than the museum.'

'You don't have to,' I protested.

'We want to,' Millicent said firmly.

In all the years I'd been coming to the West Country, I'd never had call to visit a police station before. On this holiday, I'd been inside two.

Exeter police station was situated on Waterbeer Street, a name Percy found amusing. He assumed it meant publicans on the street served watery beer. Millicent informed him that it probably meant a 'water bearing' trade was carried out there.

The city station was much larger than the one in Dawlish, but the chairs were just as uncomfortable, and it too smelt of disinfectant. Marc went to speak to the desk sergeant.

'What are you going to tell Superintendent Endicott?' Millicent whispered.

Percy gave her a withering look. 'The truth. She can't lie. Especially as Mrs Green saw her.' He turned to me. 'Why were you hiding in those bushes?'

I shrugged. 'Being nosy, I suppose. Something Harriet Green seems to share. She was in the garden, and I don't think she can be sure how much I was able to hear.'

'Say Emile turns out to be a murderer.' Percy held up his hands at the glare Millicent gave him. 'I'm not saying he is. I'm just saying we don't know the truth, and you can't go around lying to a policeman investigating a murder.'

Marc gestured for me to accompany him.

'Good luck,' Millicent whispered.

I followed Marc and a female police officer down a long corridor to an office at the back of the building. Seated next to Superintendent Endicott was Sergeant Hoxton from the night before.

The superintendent gestured for us to sit down and asked the female police constable to stay and take notes. She sat to the side of the room and rested her pocket book on her lap.

'Thank you for coming so promptly, Miss Woodmore. Mr Jansen will have explained why it's become necessary for me to talk to you yet again.' His tone made it clear he wished this could have been avoided. 'I'd like you to tell me what you were doing at

Smugglers Haunt on the afternoon of Thursday the twelfth of July and what you saw and heard.'

'I walked to Smugglers Haunt from Dawlish. I came down the driveway at the front of the house and—'

He interrupted. 'By yourself, or were your friends with you?'

'I was alone. I wasn't far from the house when I heard a car starting and moved off the driveway to the bushes at the side. Then I heard raised voices. Rupert Keats was sitting in his car, and Emile Vandamme was standing by the driver's door, talking to him through the car window. They seemed to be arguing and I stayed in the bushes so as not to embarrass them by witnessing their row.'

He raised his eyebrows at this but said nothing.

Blushing, I continued and described the argument they'd had.

'Did you hear Mr Vandamme threaten Captain Keats?'

'Not exactly. It was a flippant remark along the lines of, "If this costs me my job, you'll regret it."'

'The Keats' housekeeper, Mrs Green, seemed to think it was more serious than that.'

'It didn't sound serious to me. I think Mr Vandamme was irritated and letting off steam.'

'What happened then?'

'Captain Keats drove off, and Mr Vandamme got into his car and followed. I carried on down the driveway and knocked on the front door. Mrs Green answered.'

'Did she mention the row to you?'

I shook my head. 'She showed me into the garden, where I chatted with Mrs Keats.'

'Did she mention the row?'

I thought for a moment. 'Yes, I think she did. She was aware there had been some conflict between her husband and brother.'

'Did she seem upset by it?'

'Not particularly. She said Emile became frustrated with her husband because Captain Keats wasn't very good at his job.'

'His job as a wine merchant?'

I nodded. 'Mrs Keats said her husband lacked knowledge about the wine he stocked. That seemed to be what the argument was about. When the captain admitted he hadn't known the wine he'd supplied the hotel was the wrong vintage, Mr Vandamme suggested he employ someone who knew what they were doing.'

Superintendent Endicott considered this, then asked, 'What do you think Mr Vandamme meant when he said, "If this costs me my job, you'll regret it"?'

I shrugged. 'I've no idea. Possibly he meant that it would upset his sister if he were to be fired.'

He nodded. 'Possibly.' He glanced at Sergeant Hoxton and asked if he had any further questions. The sergeant shook his head.

'Thank you for your time, Miss Woodmore. I hope there will be no need for me to speak to you again.'

I hoped that too.

In the corridor, Marc grinned and gave me a wink, aware the WPC was behind us. 'It's obvious Mrs Green has exaggerated this argument,' he said. 'I'm going to stay here and see if I can speak to Emile.'

I nodded.

Percy and Millicent rose from the wooden seats. Percy gave the female constable a little wave and we escaped onto Waterbeer Street.

'How did it go?' Millicent asked.

'Not too bad. They don't seem to have any real evidence against Emile.'

'And you told Endicott everything you heard?' Percy asked.

'I told him the complete truth,' I assured him.

However, there was one thing I'd omitted. The idea had occurred to me when the superintendent asked what I thought Emile had meant when he'd said, "If this costs me my job, you'll regret it."

If Emile had lost his job at the Royal Clarence Hotel, he would have had to look for employment elsewhere, possibly in London. From what he'd said, he was keen to go with Marc and Annette and obviously hoped Nathalie would go too. Captain Keats would have regretted losing his wife and son if Nathalie had chosen to leave him and taken Timothy with her.

As it was, Emile hadn't lost his job but planned to join Marc and Annette in London anyway. Had he decided to remove the obstacle standing in the way of Nathalie and Timothy going with them?

20

After a late lunch, we finally set off on our delayed trip to the museum. When Percy and Millicent became embroiled in a philosophical discussion with the curator of the natural history department, I decided to nip out and call in at the nearby offices of the *Express & Echo*. I'd noticed the newspaper's fascia opposite Colson's department store when I'd been shopping with Katherine.

It was a daily newspaper and I hoped it had a well-ordered archive. My first impression of the place didn't fill me with hope. I knocked on a door badly in need of a coat of paint. No one came. I knocked again, and still no reply. It was coming up to five o'clock on a Friday, and I guessed most of the staff would have left early, but someone should still be around at this time. I tried the door handle, and it opened.

Inside, the familiar smell of printers' ink hung in the air. Hearing the sound of a typewriter, I headed down the corridor in the direction of an open door.

In the office, a young man was hammering away at the keys of a typewriter while an older man sat in a smaller adjoining office, shouting a story at him. The familiarity of the scene almost made me laugh. This was another version of myself and Elijah struggling to get the latest edition of *The Walden Herald* to the printers on time.

'What do you want?' the older man barked. He even resembled Elijah, with thinning grey hair, bloodshot eyes and a cigarette in his hand.

'I'd like to take a look at your archive, please.'

'Why?' The older man regarded me with curiosity rather than suspicion.

The young man smiled, seeming relieved by the interruption. He stretched out his fingers in the way I did when Elijah was going full pelt. Typing at speed made your hands ache.

I introduced myself and told them I worked for *The Walden Herald* and was in Devon on holiday.

'I'm Victor Satterley, and this is Bob Gullet.' He waved his cigarette at the young man at the typewriter. 'Is that what you do when you're on your holidays? Visit the offices of regional newspapers and ask to look at their archives?'

I smiled, knowing I'd have to be careful what I said to this man. He wasn't going to be fooled by the story I'd concocted about wanting to research the Keats family before the wedding. Instead, I'd tell him the truth. Or at least some of it.

I explained how we'd found skeletal remains in the cave at Smugglers Cove.

'I heard about that. The owner of the house has just died, hasn't he? Very fishy. So what is it you suspect?'

I shrugged. 'I'm just curious to know if the body we found really is Arnold Rowe.'

'Any reason to think it isn't?' Victor demanded.

'Possibly.' I wasn't about to give away too much until he agreed to my request.

He grinned. 'Alright. Let's go and have a look in the basement.' He strode out of the room, motioning for me to follow.

Bob leapt out of his chair, obviously delighted by the distraction. Victor went to the end of the corridor and opened a very low door.

'Mind your head. And be careful going down the steps. I think the wood is rotting in places.'

The smell certainly indicated rotting wood. I couldn't help feeling this wasn't an ideal place to house an archive of old newspapers.

However, once we were in the basement, I could see the newspapers were kept in large metal cabinets. In the centre of the room was a long iron table.

'Dates?' Victor demanded.

'December 1918. To start with,' I replied.

He pulled open the drawer of one of the cabinets and took out a sheaf of newspapers. He flung them onto the table.

'What are we searching for?' Bob asked.

'Any mention of Arnold Rowe.' I opened the first newspaper. 'And any mention of the Keats family or Smugglers Cove or Smugglers Haunt.'

Without a word, both Victor and Bob began to work their way through the pages of the newspapers. I guessed the rush to meet the deadline for the printers was forgotten in their pursuit of a story.

The first reference to the Keats family was the obituary for Major Laurence Keats. It gave a brief resume of his army career and it mentioned his home as Smugglers Haunt.

'Major Keats lived at Smugglers Haunt then?' Victor demanded. 'Not Captain Keats?'

I nodded, telling myself he would have found this out at some point. It wasn't until the end of December 1918 that we found an article on Arnold Rowe.

'Here you go.' Bob pushed over a copy of the *Express & Echo* dated the thirtieth of December. A short article reported the disappearance of Mr Arnold Rowe of Barton Crescent, Dawlish. His wife hadn't seen him for some weeks and had expected him to return home for Christmas. It asked if anyone had any knowledge of the whereabouts of Mr Rowe to contact Dawlish police.

Victor pulled a notebook out of his pocket and scribbled down the date of the article. 'Let's have a look to see if anyone did come forward.'

He replaced the newspapers from December 1918 in the metal cabinet and took out another bundle. He laid the pile of newspapers from January 1919 on the table.

We started to work our way through them in chronological order, and I immediately came upon an article reporting a sighting of Arnold Rowe on the fifth of January 1919. I pushed it toward Victor to read.

'Here's another.' Bob pointed to a similar article printed only days later.

I read the short column. 'So Arnold Rowe was seen on the fifth of January 1919 on Marine Parade in Dawlish. And then again on the seventh of January at Dawlish railway station.' No doubt he'd been visiting Emerald. I decided it wouldn't be fair to mention her to Bob and Victor.

Bob scratched his head. 'When exactly is this bloke supposed to have disappeared?'

'The pathologist found a train ticket in the suit pocket of the dead man. It was dated the tenth of December. The police made the assumption it was the date the man died.'

'Looks like Arnold was around some time after that, if these sightings can be trusted.' Victor scribbled down more dates in his notebook. 'That doesn't mean to say it wasn't him in the cave. It could have been an old train ticket.'

We went through the rest of the newspapers for January but found no further information on Arnold Rowe. However, a notice under 'Births, Marriages and Deaths' caught my eye.

It was the announcement of the marriage of Miss Nathalie Vandamme to Captain Rupert Keats. They'd wed at St Michael's and All Angels parish church in Dawlish on Saturday, 25 January 1919.

I remembered Nathalie telling me they'd got engaged on Armistice Day. They hadn't wasted any time in getting married.

Victor moved closer to see what I was peering at. 'Would this be the Captain Keats who died recently?'

I nodded.

Victor's beady eyes narrowed. 'So a body's found in a cave at his property. The police think it's Arnold Rowe, even though there doesn't seem much evidence to support that theory. Then a week later, Captain Keats is dead.'

I nodded.

'But his brother lived there in December 1918 when Arnold Rowe went missing?' Bob scratched his head again. 'This is getting really confusing.'

Victor drummed his fingers on the table. 'When did Captain Keats move into Smugglers Haunt?'

'After he married.'

Victor picked up the newspaper in front of me. 'Which, according to this, was in January 1919, only a month after his brother's death.'

Bob whistled. 'Something dodgy going on there, that's for sure.'

When Nathalie told me she and Rupert had moved into Smugglers Haunt after their marriage, I'd assumed it was some time after Major Keats' death. I had no idea things had moved so quickly. How must Katherine have felt, losing her husband and her home in the space of a month?

Victor was staring at me. 'How do you know all this about the Keats family?'

I shifted uncomfortably. This is where things got awkward. 'Major Laurence Keats' widow is marrying my father in a week's time.'

Victor let out a bellow of laughter. 'Are you trying to stop the wedding? I don't blame you if you are. They sound a bad lot.'

'No. Of course not.' At least, I didn't think I was. 'I don't think they are a bad lot.'

Victor eyed me sceptically. 'Don't you?'

'Well, I'm not sure about Captain Keats,' I admitted.

He tapped his notebook. 'Have they got anyone for his murder?'

I shook my head. I'd told him all I was going to for the moment. I certainly wasn't going to mention Emile, though when it came to Arnold Rowe, I was happy for him to sniff around.

'If I find out anything else about Arnold Rowe, I'll let you know,' I hesitated. 'If you hold off printing anything about the Keats family for a week, that is.'

'I'm not sure there's a story to print.' He paused. 'Yet.'

'But you know there will be.'

He nodded slowly. 'Alright. I'll hold off for now.'

21

After the drama of the previous day, I hoped Saturday's beach party would be less eventful. My father hadn't been happy about my visit to the police station.

He'd relaxed a little when Stephen had called in on his way home to inform us that Emile had been released.

But when Stephen slapped him on the back and said, 'Only a week to go until the wedding. I'm sure Iris can avoid any more encounters with Superintendent Endicott in that time,' his smile had been as weak as mine. It never paid to tempt fate.

To Millicent's delight, Horace picked us up from my grandparents' house in his chauffeur-driven Daimler. I had a feeling her glee would be shared by Emerald Dubois, who'd no doubt love the attention the car would receive when it parked outside her boarding house.

When we arrived at Marine Parade, it wasn't difficult to spot Emerald and her guests on the beach. A picnic table held a flagon of beer and numerous bottles of spirits along with an assortment of glasses. A second table was laden with dishes, including a huge pork pie, boiled eggs, salads, and plates of sandwiches.

We helped Horace with the bottles of chilled champagne he'd bought for the occasion. I hoped they hadn't come from the late Captain Keats' cellar.

Emerald was resplendent in a bright yellow and green kimono that kept flapping open to reveal a low-cut bathing suit. Judging by the strings of colourful beads around her neck and the elaborate make-up, I was pretty sure she had no intention of venturing into the sea. Her red hair gleamed in the sunshine, as did Dame Cicely's gold curls.

Most of the guests were seated on picnic blankets laid out on the sand, except Dame Cicely and Mr Andrews, who reclined on deckchairs under wide red parasols. There was no sign of Percy.

Two more deckchairs were quickly produced for Horace and Elijah, while an old khaki army blanket was thrown onto the sand at their feet for Millicent and me to sit on.

'Welcome to the Gentlemens' Bathing Cove,' Emerald said with a flourish of her hand. 'Although ladies are permitted these days. Percy tells me you're thinking of taking a dip in our bathing machine. Mr Andrews and I have set it up for you. Would you like to take a look?'

'We'd be delighted, Miss Dubois.' Horace bowed graciously.

'Where's Percy?' I asked.

Emerald gave a twirl of her beads. 'He's gone to visit his friend, Sergeant Norsworthy.' With this, she swept her kimono around her and led a bemused Horace and Elijah to inspect the bathing machine.

Millicent pulled a face. 'You don't think he's been arrested?'

'It sounds like he's gone of his own accord, though I can't imagine why.'

We went over to the beach huts to get changed, and when we emerged, I was relieved to see that Millicent's bathing costume was as ancient as mine. We wore almost identical navy and white woollen stockinette suits that had been fashionable about a decade earlier.

'I did consider buying a new costume, but I don't swim often, and it didn't seem worth the expense,' she remarked.

'Me too. I saw a lovely black crepe de chine bathing suit in *The Tatler*. I nearly sent off for it, then wondered how often I'd get to wear it.'

Self-consciously we made our way back to the party, which had grown in numbers in our brief absence. When I spotted Emile making his way towards us, accompanied by Marc and Annette and an elderly couple, I wished I had bought something a little more glamorous. Millicent quickly wrapped herself in a woollen bathing cape that must have made her extremely hot.

Emile came bounding over the sand to plant a forceful kiss on my cheek. 'Iris to my rescue yet again,' he declared.

'I think it was Marc who was your rescuer,' I replied, thinking longingly of the black crepe de chine bathing costume. It had been trimmed in a contrasting shade of jade with a bust bodice attachment. But the costume had been sixteen shillings and nine pence and the matching wrap eighteen shillings.

Emile slapped his friend on the back. He seemed unperturbed by his recent incarceration. 'True. I am lucky to have him.'

Marc and Annette smiled at him affectionately while Emile introduced the older couple as Dr and Mrs Frampton. 'My dear friends, who have been so kind to us all.'

Mrs Frampton squeezed his arm. 'We've enjoyed having you with us. We're going to miss you when you leave.'

'I will visit you often,' Emile promised.

Marc settled his wife and the Framptons on deckchairs while Emile unrolled a large towel onto the sand. Unselfconsciously, he stripped off his cotton shirt and flannel trousers.

I didn't know quite where to look, and judging by her blushes, neither did Millicent. We both took a sudden interest in what was going on with the bathing machine.

Between them, Emerald and Mr Andrews had rolled the machine down to the sea, and Horace was persuading a reluctant Elijah to climb up the stairs into it.

'Come on,' Emile called to us as he ran into the water.

Not bothering to avert our eyes this time, Millicent and I followed, taking in every inch of his muscular legs and torso.

After the initial shock of cold, it was a relief to submerge my stockinette-clad body beneath the waves. We swam out a little way, slowly becoming acclimatised to the temperature.

'It's not like Percy to miss a party. I hope he's not in any trouble,' Millicent panted.

It's what I'd been wondering. I couldn't face telling my father we'd had any more dealings with the police on this holiday. 'Why would he visit Sergeant Norsworthy?'

'Emerald didn't seem concerned, so I'm sure it's nothing to worry about.' Millicent floated on her back, spreading her arms out in the water.

That didn't reassure me. I had a feeling that Emerald was more used to being on the wrong side of the law than we were. What was of no concern to her might seem more serious to us. I pushed that thought from my mind and sank backwards to drift on the waves, enjoying the feeling of weightlessness.

Millicent and I swam a little more but mostly floated around, admiring Emile's prowess as he dived under the water, emerging suddenly beside us before swimming powerfully over to a stone jetty.

My eyes were drawn to Marc as he entered the water. I returned his smile though I felt a touch embarrassed at being caught gazing at his semi-naked body. He proved to be as strong a swimmer as Emile and we watched as they competed to see who could reach the jetty first.

Horace was also a surprisingly good swimmer, with clean, sharp strokes. Elijah was not. He floundered around in the water, gasping for breath. He seemed incapable of swimming, floating or staying upright.

When he suddenly disappeared under a wave and came up spluttering, Millicent and I went over to rescue him. Between us, we managed to haul him back into the bathing machine. We left Horace to try to revive a choking Elijah while we waded out of the water and dashed to the beach hut to change out of our waterlogged costumes.

When we returned, Elijah and Horace were attired once more in their casual flannels and seated in their deckchairs. To my relief, Percy had finally made an appearance and was playing host.

He handed chilled glasses of champagne to Horace, Millicent and me. A dazed-looking Elijah refused the champagne and accepted a large whisky. Percy insisted on bringing us food and carried over plates and various dishes so we could help ourselves before he flopped down on the khaki blanket.

Considering he was accustomed to the cuisine of the Rougemont Hotel, Horace seemed perfectly content with hard-boiled eggs, tongue sandwiches and gala pie. Elijah rejected the food and was soon demanding another whisky.

'Don't keep us in suspense, young man,' Horace said between mouthfuls. 'Why have you been fraternising with the Devonshire constabulary again?'

Percy took a swig of champagne and stretched out his long legs, clearly delighted to be asked this question. 'See that chap over there with Emerald?'

We all peered across to where Emerald was standing, her arms wrapped around a wiry man with a battered face, who looked to be in his late thirties.

'The gentleman with the black eye?' Millicent asked.

Percy waved his hand dramatically. 'That is Arnold Rowe.'

22

Millicent gasped. 'The Arnold Rowe? The dead body in the cave?'

'The very same. Although not the same as it turns out, Arnold being very much alive and living with someone called Myrtle in Salcombe.'

'Explain,' Horace ordered.

Percy did so eagerly. 'He turned up last night. Lord knows what time it was – after midnight. I was dead to the world when suddenly I heard this sharp scream. No one else seemed to have heard it, though Dame Cicely and Mr Andrews knocked back a fair amount of claret after their return from the theatre. Anyway, I crept downstairs to find the front door wide open and Emerald in the hallway with this chap dressed in black. He had his hand over her mouth. I hadn't thought to grab a weapon, but it didn't look like he had one either, so I squared up to him and—'

'You gave him that black eye?' Millicent exclaimed.

'No, that came later.' Percy waved off the interruption. 'I told him to get his mitts off her.'

'And did he?' I asked.

'Oh yes. He let her go and apologised. He said he'd only done it to stop her from screaming the place down.'

'How considerate of him,' Horace remarked.

'I thought he seemed a decent chap,' Percy agreed. 'Though I could appreciate why Emerald kicked him in the shin. I asked what was going on and Emerald said, "This is Arnie." I said, "Pleased to meet you, Arnie," not immediately cottoning on. I was still half asleep. Then she says, "This is Arnold. Arnold Rowe."'

'And what did Mr Rowe want?' Elijah was now looking more like his normal self, with a cigarette in one hand and a whisky in the other.

'He said he'd heard he was dead and wanted to check if it was true. We went into the kitchen, Emerald got out the brandy, and I told him what had been going on.'

'Why did he disappear without a word?' I asked.

'He couldn't face living with his wife any more. So he did a bunk.'

'Where has Mr Rowe been?' Horace seemed to be enjoying the entertainment as much as the food and drink.

'Living in Salcombe with this woman called Myrtle. They call themselves Mr and Mrs Brown. Emerald seemed to be quite miffed about this and—'

I glanced at Arnold's black eye. 'And she thumped him?'

'No, that came later.' Percy waved off the interruption again. 'Where was I? Oh yes, apparently Myrtle used to run a boarding house on Marine Parade too. She and Emerald were rivals – and not just in business. Emerald was delighted when Myrtle sold up and moved away, not realising she'd taken Arnold with her.'

'I imagine things were getting too hot in town for him.' Elijah drained the last of his whisky and accepted the glass of champagne Percy offered him. 'You say his wife lives in Dawlish too?

Mr Rowe doesn't appear to travel far. Salcombe must have been quite a departure for him.'

'Rather too much nefarious activity on his own doorstep,' Horace agreed, holding out his glass for a top-up.

Percy nodded as he filled Horace's glass. 'I ended up feeling quite sorry for the chap.'

'What about his poor wife!' Millicent exclaimed. 'Not knowing whether he was dead or alive.'

'He seems scared of her. Hence, turning up at the Jewel of the Sea in the middle of the night dressed as a burglar. He didn't want to be seen but was desperate to know what was going on and decided to trust Emerald.'

I sipped my champagne. 'Will he go to the police?'

'He was reluctant at first. He said he'd rather go back to the trenches than return home to Mrs Rowe. Seemed a trifle unkind, but I haven't met the woman, so I can't really comment. When Emerald told him that Mrs Rowe was keen to marry the ironmonger chap and would probably agree to a divorce, he seemed to reconsider. I told him it was shabby behaviour to leave another fellow in a grave with his name on it. He admitted that wouldn't be fair and said he'd go and see Sergeant Norsworthy.'

I smiled. 'I wish I could have been there to see that.'

'I went with him to the police station. That's why I'm late. I didn't trust him not to do a bunk again.' Percy grinned. 'The look on Norsworthy's face was a sight to behold. And then—'

'Sergeant Norsworthy didn't give him that black eye, did he?' Millicent asked in a shocked voice.

'No. Will you stop interrupting?' Percy said in exasperation.

'We will if you tell us who gave him the black eye,' I said reasonably.

'His wife. News of his return was all over town by the time we left the police station. We were walking back to Emerald's when

Mrs Rowe appeared and gave him one hell of a clout. He went down like a sack of spuds.'

Horace and Elijah chuckled.

Percy got up to fetch us more food and came back with cold ham, chicken and slices of pie.

We ate for a while, then Millicent said, 'So who is the man we found in the cave?' Her brow creased. 'This proves we were right about Sergeant Norsworthy not investigating properly.'

Elijah lit a cigarette. 'I've always suspected it was a Belgian refugee. It would account for no one reporting him missing, and he was wearing a suit made in Belgium.'

I nodded. 'He must have been staying somewhere in Teignmouth and took the train to Dawlish.'

'But why Smugglers Haunt?' Horace waved a chicken drumstick. 'That's the question.'

'He was exploring the Devon coastline,' Percy suggested between mouthfuls of pie. 'Perhaps he'd heard of old Dick Endicott and decided to explore Smugglers Cove. Like us, he probably didn't know the beach was private land.'

I pulled a face. 'In December? More likely he went to visit someone at Smugglers Haunt, Major or Mrs Keats?'

'Not necessarily,' Elijah argued. 'Mrs Green lived there too. And from what you've told us, Rupert Keats was there most days. Arnold and Joyce Rowe also both spent a lot of time there, as did Stephen and Gwen Damerell and Dr Frampton.'

'Or his visit could have nothing to do with any of them. He could simply have become confused and got lost,' Millicent said.

I didn't think this was likely. 'Did you ask Arnold about Rupert Keats?'

Percy nodded. 'He told me Keats was always keen to get his hands on any duty-free booze he could sell on at full price. But as Owen told us, the boats had stopped coming in during the war, and it wasn't easy to start it up again. Arnold said there was nothing left for him around here, so he sneaked off with Myrtle.'

We carried on eating and the conversation petered out as Elijah began to doze off. It wasn't long before both he and Horace were snoozing in their deckchairs. Percy moved the parasol to give them shade and we began to clear up.

I was helping Percy and Millicent carry the dirty plates and glasses back to the Jewel of the Sea when I noticed that Emile, Marc and Annette had finished their picnic and were heading into the water. The Framptons were sitting alone watching them. It was time to try to dispel some of my fears about Katherine.

I dumped the crockery in the sink, leaving Millicent to do the washing up and Percy the drying, saying I'd bring in some of the uneaten food to store in the larder.

On the beach, I went over to where the Framptons were seated in their deckchairs and asked if they'd like anything to drink.

'Nothing more for us, my dear,' the doctor replied.

Mrs Frampton smiled up at me. 'Are you looking forward to your father's wedding? It's next Saturday, isn't it?'

It was the cue I needed. 'Yes. And I'm looking forward to spending more time with Katherine.' I sat in the deckchair Annette had vacated. 'You must know her well?'

'I've known Katherine since she was a girl,' Dr Frampton said. 'It's good to see her settled. Her late husband, Major Keats, was a fine man. She was devastated when he died.'

'It took her a long time to recover,' Mrs Frampton added. 'I'm glad she's found happiness.'

'His death must have come as a shock. I believe his condition was improving at one stage?'

I'd remembered Stephen Damerell saying it seemed Laurence Keats might get better, then his health had deteriorated.

The doctor shook his head. 'I've seen it before. The patient looks like they're rallying but I knew the gas had taken too great a toll on Laurence. It was clear when he returned from France he wouldn't survive. Katherine and Rupert did their best for him, and he only lived as long as he did because of their care. I was with him at the end and he was as comfortable as he could be.'

'How sad.' I felt guilty for raising the subject. Had I really thought Katherine could have been involved in her first husband's death? I had to admit, it had crossed my mind. I justified my questioning by saying that it was Rupert that I'd been suspicious of. After all, he'd been the one to gain from his brother's death.

It was clear that Major Keats had died of natural causes. But that didn't change the fact that someone had turned up at Smugglers Cove and ended up dead in the cave. And it wasn't Arnold Rowe.

23

Glad no one had witnessed my conversation with the Framptons, especially Elijah, I joined Millicent in a barefoot stroll along the beach. She'd decided we ought to keep an eye on Percy, who'd returned from the Jewel of the Sea in a fashionable swimsuit and plunged straight into the water.

After the boozy lunch, Millicent was worried he might drown. I admired his constitution and if I'd invested in the crepe de chine swimsuit would have been tempted to join him. As it was, neither Millicent nor I could face putting on our damp stockinette costumes again.

I paddled in the shallows while Millicent watched the swimmers with a rapt expression. Then I realised it wasn't Percy she was looking at. It was Emile. I got the impression some sort of competition was going on.

'What are they doing?'

'Seeing who can swim from the rock to the jetty fastest.'

'Oh dear. I assume Percy's losing?'

She nodded.

Percy was a good swimmer, but Emile was stronger. When he

waded out of the water, Millicent wasn't the only one who couldn't take her eyes off his chiselled physique. I glanced around and noticed most of the women on the beach were looking in our direction.

Percy followed Emile out of the sea, trying not to show how out of breath he was. I threw towels at them both, and Emile made a show of thanking me, I suspect to annoy Percy. I could feel Millicent's envious stare as he bestowed a soggy kiss on my cheek. I could also sense Percy's displeasure.

'You are my guardian angel,' Emile purred. 'Always there to take care of me when I need you.'

Percy gave a derisive snort. I didn't blame him. No one had ever described me as an angel before. Even I had to admit it wasn't the most accurate portrayal of my character.

'Why don't you come back to the Jewel of the Sea to get changed?' came a silky voice. Emerald tossed her bright red curls and gazed at Emile from under her eyelashes.

'Thank you, Emerald.' He blew a kiss in her direction.

We crossed the bridge over the railway line, Emerald blatantly staring at Emile in his bathing shorts, while Millicent and I sneaked glances when we thought Percy wasn't looking.

Emerald opened the front door and said to Emile, 'I'm sure Percy won't mind you using his room to change. I'll fix us some drinks after I've cleared up.'

'Thank you, Percee,' Emile said, a mischievous glint in his eyes.

Percy scowled and climbed the stairs, with Emile in tow, three pairs of eyes following the movements of his highly toned legs. They must have bumped into Dame Cicely on the landing as I heard her regal voice declaring, 'How delicious,' before she swept down the stairs.

Horace and Elijah were propping up the bar in the lounge

with Mr Andrews. Emerald had already given them a tour of the cave, and they were now sampling some of her 'imported' French brandy. Dame Cicely accepted the glass Horace offered and was enticed into revealing salacious gossip about some of the more famous actors and actresses she'd worked with over the years.

Millicent and I went with Emerald into the kitchen to help clear up. When I passed the open back door, I noticed Arnold Rowe sitting on a wooden crate in the back yard, holding a slice of cucumber over his black eye.

Emerald thrust a teacloth into my hand and asked me to dry the dishes and stack them on the sideboard. Millicent had the unenviable task of drying glasses and carrying them on a tray to the bar. I'd never seen such an array of wine, cocktail and shot glasses, along with whisky tumblers and champagne flutes.

'Do you get many people staying here in winter?' I asked Emerald, who was scrubbing the kitchen table, her strings of beads leaving trails in the suds.

'Not so much holidaymakers – more people wanting lodgings in the south over the winter months. Some of my variety performers come to me for a rest. They only do the summer season, it pays the best, then they have a few months off in the winter. Sometimes I take in the cast of touring productions.'

'Do you remember hearing about anyone disappearing from their lodgings around Christmas 1918?'

She laughed. 'I barely remember last week, let alone five years ago. I can have a look in my old books to see if I got any warnings.'

'Warnings?'

'Of absconders. Some guests up and leave without paying. They move on to other lodgings and do the same there. When that happens, we tell the police and other boarding house owners, so they can keep an eye out for them. Rarely get your money back, but it can stop them from pulling the same trick on someone else. We all keep our little black books. I'll see if I can find my old one.'

'Thank you, that would be helpful.'

'Is Arnold still out there?' she asked.

I peered out of the back door and nodded.

'Take this out to him, would you?' She handed me a bottle of beer.

I went out to Arnold, who took the cucumber from his eye and regarded me glumly. I gave him the beer.

'You look better than when I last saw you.'

He stared at me in confusion, and I explained that my friends and I had found the skeleton that was supposed to have been him.

He laughed. 'Poor sod. I shouldn't be sitting here feeling sorry for myself, should I?'

'Do you have any idea who the man in the cave might be?' I sat down on a wooden crate next to him.

'Not a clue.' He took a long slurp of beer.

'Did you know about the cave?'

He shook his head. 'I used to do odd jobs at Smugglers Haunt, but I didn't go down to the cove much. Had no reason to.'

'You didn't see anyone on the beach or hanging around the house?'

'Not at that time of the year. It can get bloody cold down there in winter.'

'Sergeant Norsworthy seemed to think the caves were used for smuggling.'

He laughed. 'Perhaps he thinks old Dick Endicott is still bringing in boats full of gold. No one's going to pull in there with crates full of liquor and slog up the cliff with them.'

'Is that what Captain Keats wanted you to do?'

He gave me a sharp look. 'Who told you that?'

'Owen Locke. I'm not interested in getting anyone into any trouble. I'm just curious to know what Rupert Keats had been planning.'

'To be honest with you, it was one of the reasons why I left. That and my wife.' He raised a hand to his bruised eye.

I nodded sympathetically. 'Rupert made you leave?'

'I wanted to get away from him as well as Joyce. He had some daft idea that I could bring in crate-loads of wine that he'd be able to sell in his shop. I went along with it at first. I knew I could pick up the odd bottle from Emerald. I wanted to keep him sweet as my aunt was his brother's housekeeper, and I didn't want to make things awkward for her.'

'But Rupert wanted more?'

'He couldn't get enough. He suggested I take a boat and go over to France. It was a ridiculous plan. I'd have bloody drowned. In the end, I got fed up with everything and did a bunk.'

'Do you remember witnessing Major Keats' signature in October 1918?'

'Signature on what? I didn't see the major much. He was very sick.'

'You and your aunt are supposed to have witnessed the major signing a codicil that he'd added to his will. Your signatures are on the document.'

He screwed up his face as if trying to remember. 'That's right. I didn't actually see the major sign it. His signature was already there. I just did what my aunt told me to. I didn't really know what it was, but I didn't see any harm in it.' He grew wary. 'Am I in trouble?'

I shook my head. 'It's not your fault if it wasn't explained to you properly. You signed to say you'd seen Major Keats in person write his signature. But that clearly wasn't the case, was it?'

He shrugged. 'I trusted my aunt. She'd do anything for Major and Captain Keats.'

Including falsifying a will, I was tempted to say. Instead, I asked, 'Will you go and see Mrs Green?'

He nodded. 'Now Captain Keats is dead, I can show my face at Smugglers Haunt again. I hope she's not too angry with me for running off.' He touched his eye. 'I don't want another one of these.'

'Then what will you do?'

'I've got to sort things out with Joyce before I can go back to Salcombe.' He sighed. 'She wants a divorce. God knows how I go about that. It was much simpler being dead.'

I thought for a moment. 'Do you know Stephen Damerell?'

'The solicitor that lives at Primrose Lodge? Yeah, he's helped me out a few times.'

'It might be a good idea for you to go and see him. If you tell him what you've just told me about how you came to witness Major Keats' signature, I'm sure he'd be willing to advise you how to proceed with a divorce.' Stephen would be delighted by Arnold's reappearance, especially when he heard that Arnold hadn't seen Major Keats sign the will. It was one step closer to proving Katherine should have inherited Smugglers Haunt.

He nodded slowly. 'I might just do that.'

'And if you want to earn a few bob, go and see Victor Satterley at the *Express & Echo* and tell him I sent you. He'd probably be willing to pay you a modest amount for your exclusive tale of how you came back from the dead.'

24

On Sunday morning, Millicent and I took the train back to Dawlish. She went in search of Percy while I trudged up Bere Hill to pay a call on the Damerells at Primrose Lodge.

Stephen opened the door, Bruno, the Labrador, at his heels. I followed him into the family room at the back of the house.

'Did Arnold Rowe come to see you?' I asked.

He grinned. 'He did indeed. It's what I thought all along. Rupert fraudulently added that codicil to the will. Arnold didn't even know what he was signing though I suspect his aunt, Harriet Green, knew perfectly well what she was doing.'

'What are you going to do?' I settled into a comfy chair by the window, Bruno lolling at my feet.

'Challenge it. But Katherine wants me to wait. I can see her point. It wouldn't be fair to land this on Nathalie after what's happened.'

'Why do you think Rupert did it?' I leant down to stroke Bruno's ears.

'To win Nathalie.' Gwen came into the room and sat down opposite. 'He was besotted with her.'

'How did she feel about him?' I was curious as to why Nathalie had married a man so much older than herself. And so quickly. I could understand Rupert's eagerness to lay claim to his inheritance and his bride. But Nathalie... Why had she been willing to go along with it?

Gwen considered this. 'I think she wanted a home. A place to feel settled. Who could blame her after what she'd been through? Rupert made it clear he'd do anything for her.'

I nodded. 'Nathalie said that when Rupert proposed, he told her he'd inherit Smugglers Haunt when Laurence died. That was on Armistice Day.'

'Did he?' Stephen pursed his lips. 'Never liked the chap.'

Gwen was more sympathetic. 'Rupert did care for his brother, I'm sure of that. Laurence was the last of his close family. I think that's why he was so keen to get engaged to Nathalie. He wanted a family of his own.' She looked at her husband. 'Maybe Laurence knew this and decided to leave him the house.'

Stephen shook his head. 'If that had been the case, Laurence would have said something to Katherine. He wouldn't have just changed his will without telling her.'

Gwen nodded. 'I think Rupert was a weak man, rather than a bad one. Nathalie probably thought she could mould him into what she wanted. Unfortunately, he had no head for business. He certainly wasn't as wealthy as he led her to believe.'

Is that why Nathalie was so interested in divorce laws, I wondered. Had she wanted to divorce Rupert but been unable to prove his infidelity? It sounded like Rupert's fling with Emerald hadn't amounted to much. With a lack of evidence, could Nathalie have chosen a different way to get rid of him?

'You say he wasn't a bad man. But did he have anything to do with that chap ending up in the cave?' Stephen asked.

Gwen appeared shocked. 'No. What reason could he have?'

That was the question. 'Katherine said you both visited Laurence when he was ill. Did you notice anything out of the ordinary at Smugglers Haunt? Did any visitors turn up unexpectedly?'

They both shook their heads.

'All our attention was on Laurence,' Gwen said.

Stephen nodded. 'It was sad to see him cut down that way.'

I ruffled Bruno's ears, thinking about the train ticket found in the man's pocket. With Arnold Rowe's reappearance, it seemed the date on the ticket probably was an accurate indication of when the man had died.

* * *

I left Primrose Lodge and strolled through the town to Marine Parade. I spotted Percy and Millicent on the sea wall and was about to join them when I saw Emerald waving at me from the window of the Jewel of the Sea.

The door to the boarding house was opened before I reached it.

'I've found something for you.' Emerald picked up a padded record book from the hall table. 'I've been going through my old black books and there was an absconder around the time you mentioned.'

'From lodgings in Dawlish?'

'Teignmouth.' She pointed to an entry in large, looped handwriting.

I felt a rush of excitement. The train ticket in the man's pocket had been a return from Teignmouth.

'I've written it down.' Emerald handed me a scrap of paper. 'Agatha Challacombe. Everyone calls her Aggy. She runs the Pier

View boarding house on Den Crescent. She had a gentleman go missing in December 1918.'

I thanked her and rushed to the front door.

'Tell her you're a friend of mine,' Emerald called after me.

Percy readily agreed to drive us to Teignmouth. It was only when we got there we realised we didn't have a local map or any idea where Den Crescent was.

Millicent sensibly pointed out that Pier View boarding house was probably in the vicinity of the pier. And she was right.

As well as a view of the pier, the boarding house was only a short distance from the Assembly Rooms. Teignmouth had been a fashionable seaside resort in the Georgian era, and most of the seafront buildings dated from that time. The stylish Georgian architecture of the Assembly Rooms was reflected in the nearby houses, including the three-storey Pier View boarding house.

We knocked on the white-painted front door, and a cheery-looking woman of about sixty answered. 'Sorry, dears. All my rooms are taken.'

Percy explained that he was staying with Emerald at the Jewel of the Sea boarding house in Dawlish and that she'd sent us. 'We're searching for someone who might have stayed with you about five years ago.'

'Come in, and I'll see if I can help.' She showed us into a bright, spacious room at the front of the house. 'All the guests are out, so we can talk here.'

I couldn't help comparing the pristine lounge of Pier View, with its white armchair slipcovers and scent of lavender water, to the pub-like lounge of the Jewel of the Sea. We sat in solid armchairs, careful not to touch the spotless slipcovers.

'Emerald told us that one of your guests left without paying in December 1918,' I said. 'Would you have a record of his name?'

'Jean? I remember him well. A Belgian gentleman.' She shook

her head sadly. 'I've often wondered what became of him. I asked the other boarding houses to look out for him because I was worried about him. Not because I thought he was an absconder. I've been in this business long enough to know the type.'

I had a sense of anticipation that I could see Millicent and Percy shared.

'Jean? Do you remember his surname?'

She screwed up her face. 'I can't. It will be in my book. Was this gentleman a friend of yours?'

'Not exactly...' I wasn't sure how to explain it.

Millicent decided to be honest and told Aggy how she'd come across the body in the cave.

Aggy's hand went to her mouth. 'And you think it could be Jean?'

'He had a return train ticket from Teignmouth in his pocket dated the tenth of December,' I said.

'Oh my goodness, the poor man. I was afraid something had happened to him.'

'Did you inform the police?'

'Pah.' Aggy scowled. 'They weren't interested. I didn't want to get Jean into trouble, but I was worried when he didn't come back.'

'You didn't think he'd just run off without paying?' Millicent asked.

'As I said, he didn't seem the type. You get to know these things. He looked so thin, I thought he might have been taken ill. And he'd left all his things behind.'

Percy pushed his floppy hair back over his brow. 'Didn't the police find it odd that he'd left all his belongings here?'

'The trouble was, he didn't have much with him when he arrived. They said he probably found whoever he was searching for and didn't bother coming back for his few clothes.'

'He was trying to find someone?' I leant forward, eager to learn more. 'Did he say who?'

'I can't remember. I think he'd come from London to try to locate friends in this region.'

'What did he look like?' Millicent's sorrowful expression showed she believed Jean was our man.

'Tall, dark-haired. Late twenties, early thirties. It's possible he was younger, but he looked haggard. I got the impression he'd suffered. Either he'd been ill, or the war had taken its toll. I had a feeling he'd spent a long time fighting.'

'What was he wearing when you last saw him?' I thought of the skeletal hand protruding from the sleeve of the brown suit.

'I think he only had the one suit. It was brown tweed.'

'Poor Jean.' Millicent became tearful.

Aggy seemed just as upset. 'You think it was Jean you found?'

She nodded.

'I don't understand how he ended up in the cave? How did he die?'

'We're not sure,' Millicent replied. 'It might have been a rock fall.'

I could understand her reluctance to explain our suspicions to Aggy.

'Did Jean wear a ring?' I asked.

'Yes!' Aggy exclaimed. 'Now you mention it, that does ring a bell. Silver with some engraving on it. I only remember because it looked valuable yet all his clothing was shabby and he had a tatty old bag. I thought it must be precious to him otherwise he'd have pawned or sold it.'

'Was it etched with tiny doves?'

Aggy shook her head. 'I couldn't say.'

Millicent was now dabbing her eyes, and Percy reached out and put his arm around her shoulder.

Aggy got up stiffly and walked to the door. 'I think Jean had already suffered. Stay here. I'll get my Rita to bring you some tea while I see if I can find my register for that year.'

We sat in silence, staring out of the window at the holidaymakers on the pier.

Rita came bustling in with a tray of tea and biscuits. She was a younger version of Aggy. 'I'll leave you to serve yourselves. Mum won't be long,' she said cheerily.

We thanked her and Percy poured Millicent a cup of tea.

She sniffed. 'It's silly to feel upset over someone I didn't even know.'

'No, it's not.' He patted her hand. 'This poor chap probably spent years fighting, separated from his family and friends and then ends up dead in a cave. It makes me feel sad thinking about it.'

'Me too.' Although I was pleased we'd discovered the identity of the man, just knowing his name made it even more wretched.

Aggy returned with an open book in her hands. She showed us the entry.

'Jean Claes,' Millicent said in a low voice.

Apart from his name and the date of his arrival, which was the eighth of December, there was no other information.

'What did you do with Mr Claes' belongings?' I asked.

'There wasn't much. He only had one bag. I packed his clothes and bits and bobs in it.'

'Do you still have the bag?' Percy took a biscuit and nibbled slowly, careful not to drop any crumbs.

Aggy screwed up her face. 'I can't rightly say. It might be in the attic. I'll have a search, and if I find it, I'll send a note to Emerald. What's happened to Jean's body?'

We exchanged glances, and I told her about Sergeant Norsworthy's assumption that the man was Arnold Rowe.

She snorted. 'What a gawcum.'

I wasn't sure what gawcum meant, but I could hazard a guess. Percy seemed delighted by the word. I hoped he wasn't going to start using it.

'We should tell Superintendent Endicott about this.' Millicent put her teacup back on the tray. 'Mr Claes may have a family in Belgium who have been missing him all these years.'

Aggy agreed. 'I'm happy to tell the police everything I've told you.'

We left the boarding house and walked along the pier, our sombre mood in contrast to the lively holidaymakers around us. We'd thanked Aggy and promised to tell her anything more we discovered about Jean Claes.

'It sounds like this chap was in a bad way. Perhaps his death was natural causes.' Percy dug his hands deep in his pockets.

'Why did he end up in a cave at Smugglers Cove?' Millicent said.

'Katherine told me about the work she did during the war, interviewing the refugees for the war office. It's possible Jean went to Smugglers Haunt to see her,' I replied, speculating aloud.

Percy frowned. 'How would he know where to find her? Are you suggesting she's involved in his death?'

'All I'm saying is he might have hoped she could help him find his friends.'

It crossed my mind that perhaps Katherine had been seeing this man, although I wasn't about to share this suspicion with Millicent and Percy. Aggy had said she thought Jean had come to Devon from London. Katherine must have come into contact with hundreds of refugees during the course of the war. Had she met Jean at some point and become involved with him? He would have been around ten or even fifteen years younger, but there might have been an affair. She would have had ample opportunity with the major away. Perhaps she thought she'd seen the last of him and then he turned up unannounced at her home. She would have wanted to protect her dying husband from any confrontations. Maybe drugging Jean and putting him in the cave was her only way of doing that.

'What about her husband, Major Keats?' Millicent suggested. 'Could he have gone there to see him?'

'It's possible, I suppose, although the major was very ill at that time.'

'Maybe he didn't call at Smugglers Haunt at all,' Percy argued. 'He could have gone down the same cliff path as us to explore the beach and ended up in the cave. If the weather was bad, he might have taken shelter there, then there was a rock fall.'

'What do we do now?' Millicent asked.

I pondered. 'I think I should speak to Katherine about Jean Claes and see what she says. And if Stephen's home, I can ask him to talk to Superintendent Endicott for us.' I did not want to pay another visit to Waterbeer Street.

Millicent nodded. 'That seems the best course of action.'

25

On returning to Dawlish, Percy dropped Millicent off at the train station before driving me to Primrose Lodge. We'd decided it would be best for me to talk to Katherine alone and get the train back to Exeter later.

Before I got out of the car, I said to Percy, 'Do you think Katherine could have been seeing Jean Claes?'

He stared at me in dismay. 'No, I don't. Why would you think that?'

'Because I find it odd that she would leave her husband when he was so ill to spend time in their London flat. Aggy said she thought this man had travelled to Devon from London. Perhaps he came looking for Katherine?'

He sighed in exasperation. 'Katherine was in London on the tenth of December.'

'We've only got her word for that. She could have been at home. What if she was seeing this man and when he turned up on her doorstep, she panicked and killed him?'

'And dragged him down to the cove on her own?'

'Aggy said he was thin.'

'Yes, thin and ill. You think Katherine was having an affair with an emaciated man from Belgium? You don't think it's more likely he'd been away fighting and was searching for loved ones he'd lost contact with?'

Put like that, he had a point.

'It was just a thought.' I opened the car door.

Before I could get out, Percy grabbed my arm. 'Your father is getting married in six days' time. Please reconcile yourself to it. For your own sake.'

I pulled away and slammed the door closed. He gazed at me for a moment, then drove away.

Annoyed with myself – and Percy – I marched up the path and rapped on the door of Primrose Lodge. Gwen welcomed me with her usual affability and said Katherine was in the garden. She discreetly left us to chat.

'Iris. How lovely to see you. Did you enjoy your beach party?' Katherine's pleasure at seeing me caused a pang of guilt.

I told her about the party, watching her eyes crinkle with laughter when I described Elijah's ill-fated attempt at sea swimming. I had to admit, I could see why my father was attracted to her. She had a lovely face with rich hazel eyes, a freckled nose and a smile that brought dimples to her cheeks. I could also appreciate how he'd fallen for her warm personality. The question was, when had he succumbed to her charms?

The suspicion that she might have been having an affair while Laurence was sick was still in my mind. If not Jean Claes, had she been spending time in London to see my father?

After I'd finished my account of the beach party, I casually got to the reason I was there, mentioning that Emerald had told us about a man who'd gone missing from a boarding house in December 1918.

'Really?' she said with interest. 'Do you know his name?'

I watched her closely when I told her he was called Jean Claes and was from Belgium.

She gave no sign of recognition. 'I've never heard of him.'

'Could he have come looking for you at Smugglers Haunt?'

'It's possible, I suppose. Although refugees were going home then, not arriving. The centres had all closed, and most of the volunteers had stood down.'

'Do you remember any new foreign visitors to Dawlish around that time?'

She shook her head. 'I didn't have any direct contact with refugees after the war. I still went into London, but it was all paperwork by that stage. Sometimes I'd stay at the flat for a few days.'

'Did you see my father during that time?' I blurted it out before I could stop myself.

She looked taken aback by the question. 'No.' Her relaxed manner turned colder and more tense. 'Thomas and Elijah came to see me after Laurence died. We weren't seeing each other before then if that's what you think.'

'Oh, no, I didn't mean it like that,' I lied. It was exactly what I'd meant.

'I was busy caring for Laurence. I remember seeing your father later the following year. That's when he told me he was keen for you to move back to Walden. He hoped you'd feel more settled there.'

So my father had discussed me with Katherine sometime in 1919, yet the first I'd known of her existence was when I'd met her in Paris towards the end of 1921. I swallowed my irritation and returned to the possibly safer subject of Smugglers Haunt.

'Could Jean Claes have been visiting your husband, Major Keats?'

'I can't think why. Laurence was too ill to see anyone. We

didn't encourage visitors at that time as he needed peace and quiet.' She spoke more softly and seemed warier.

'If Jean Claes had called in your absence, who would he have seen?'

'Probably Mrs Green. I doubt she would have invited him in. She was very protective of Laurence.'

'How long have you known Mrs Green?'

The look she gave me told me she was becoming unhappy at my relentless questioning. 'Harriet Green has been at Smugglers Haunt for as long as anyone can remember. She's devoted to the Keats family. She worked as housekeeper for Laurence's parents. When they died in 1910, he inherited Smugglers Haunt, and we moved there.'

I could feel her tension yet I couldn't stop myself from asking, 'You said Rupert spent a lot of time at Smugglers Haunt when Laurence was ill? Could he have arranged to meet Jean Claes there?'

'It's possible, although I can't think why he'd meet him at the villa. He had his own place in Exeter. Do you suspect him of something? Or me?' she asked bluntly.

I gave a forced laugh. 'I'm sorry. I didn't mean to sound so suspicious. Elijah's always telling me off for reading too many detective stories.'

In fact, I wasn't sure who I suspected. I couldn't see why Rupert would be associated with Jean Claes. From what Katherine had told me about her war work, she was the one more likely to have known him. I was curious to see how she'd react when I said we planned to go to the police with what we'd found out.

'I was going to ask Stephen's advice about approaching Superintendent Endicott.'

She seemed unperturbed. 'I'm sure he'll advise you to speak

to the police for the sake of this man's family. They might be able to trace them. You should also talk to Nathalie and Annette. They would know about the Belgian community in Dawlish and Exeter at that time.'

'Good idea.' I decided it would be prudent to change the subject rather than risk upsetting her further, and asked her about the seating plans for the wedding reception. The conversation continued more harmoniously after that. However, by her appraising expression, I don't think Katherine was fooled by my sudden interest in the wedding arrangements.

* * *

When I got to Exeter, I took Katherine's advice and paid a call at the Jansens' flat before returning to my grandparents.

Marc opened the door. 'Iris.' He lowered his voice. 'Has something happened? Emile and Nathalie are here.'

I shook my head. He looked relieved and showed me into the lounge of the basement flat. Packing cases were lined against one wall, half filled with books and ornaments wrapped in old newspaper.

'Iris, we're just about to have dinner,' Annette said. 'Would you like to join us?'

I declined, saying I was expected back at my grandparents. 'I'm sorry to disturb you. I won't stay long. I wanted to ask you a question. Have any of you ever heard of a man called Jean Claes? Either here or in Belgium?'

I watched their faces closely but could see no flicker of recognition. Annette seemed nervous, but that wasn't unusual.

Nathalie was her usual cool self. 'Who is Jean Claes?' she asked.

'It's likely he was the man we found at Smugglers Cove. I wonder if perhaps Captain Keats knew him?'

'Emerald told me about Arnold Rowe showing up.' Emile laughed. 'Norsworthy must feel a fool.'

Nathalie shook her head. 'I never heard Rupert mention the name. It's possible he was a business contact, although I think he would have told me about him if this man was Belgian.'

'You'd been discharged from the army by December 1918, hadn't you?' I said to Emile and Marc. I tried to make it sound casual, but Emile gave me an odd look.

His eyes narrowed. 'Do you suspect us of something?'

I smiled, trying to temper my words. 'Of course not. I just wondered if someone might have come here searching for you?'

'We came back to England the month before,' Marc replied. 'I don't recall anyone else arriving from Belgium at that time.'

'Most of our fellow countrymen were returning home,' Annette added.

I left them to their dinner and escaped from the flat before I aroused any more animosity. My insistent questioning was doing nothing for my popularity.

I was frustrated that none of them, including Katherine, had shown any hint of recognising the name Jean Claes.

I realised how desperate I was to solve this mystery. I couldn't stand the thought of not knowing what happened to Jean – or who killed Rupert Keats. But I was going home on Monday the thirtieth of July, and it was likely I'd leave Devon with unanswered questions.

26

When Percy turned up on the doorstep on Monday morning, Nan practically dragged him in for breakfast, despite his protests that he'd already eaten.

He joined us in the dining room and waited until she'd returned to the kitchen before whispering, 'Aggy's grandson turned up on his bicycle this morning with a note. She's found Jean's bag up in the attic.'

Millicent put down her toast. 'Should we tell Superintendent Endicott?'

'Once we've looked in it.' I gulped down my tea. 'I was planning to call in at Damerell & Tate's later to see Stephen. I'll let him know if we find anything.'

Percy grinned. 'Why did I think you'd say that? My car's outside. Teignmouth it is then.'

He parked outside the Assembly Rooms again and went over to a poster advertising a dancing competition. He turned to us. 'Who'd like to be my partner?'

Millicent pulled a face.

'Why don't you ask Emerald?' I suggested.

'Her ankles.' He scanned the other posters with interest. 'What about seeing *The Comedy Players*?'

Millicent and I ignored him, more interested in seeing Jean's bag. I suspected Millicent wouldn't relish an evening of seaside variety acts.

We knocked on the door of the Pier View boarding house and Aggy answered.

'Come through to the back parlour. I've got guests in the lounge.'

She ushered us into a private room at the back of the house. On the table was a large duffel bag made of thick canvas. Its dull brown colour didn't disguise the stains and scuffs. The bag was clearly well travelled and smelt of engine oil.

'Do you mind if we take a look?' I asked.

'You go ahead. I'll be back in a moment. I've got to see our Rita before she goes to the shops.'

I opened the bag and tipped the items into a pile on the table.

Millicent stood back. 'It feels wrong to go through this man's private things.'

'I must say, it does seem a bit nosy.' Percy stood with his hands in his pockets, peering at the heap of belongings.

Ignoring them, I examined the clothing then carefully placed each item back into the bag. What was left was a shaving kit and a notebook. I flicked through the tattered pages. Most of the writing was in Dutch – there were only six words written in English and my breath caught when I read them: Mrs Katherine Keats, Smugglers Haunt, Dawlish.

I held out the open page so Millicent and Percy could see.

'Oh,' Millicent said uncertainly, sharing a glance with Percy, who was silent. I closed the notebook, placed it on top of the neatly packed clothes and shut the bag.

When Aggy returned, I asked, 'Did Jean ever mention Mrs Katherine Keats to you?'

Aggy shook her head. 'Not that I recall.'

'What about Nathalie Vandamme, Emile Vandamme, Marc Jansen or Annette Jansen?'

She shook her head again. 'I'm sorry. They don't ring any bells.'

'Could we take this?' I gestured to the bag. 'I'd like to give it to Mr Stephen Damerell, a solicitor who's advising us. He'll pass it on to Superintendent Endicott.'

'Please do. I hope it will help them locate Jean's family.'

We thanked Aggy, and Percy carried the bag out to the car.

'Shouldn't we take it straight to the police?' Millicent said.

I sighed. 'If we do that, I run the risk of Elijah accusing me of trying to implicate Katherine.'

I was aware there were only five days until the wedding. As much as I wanted to find out the truth about Katherine's relationship with Jean Claes, I didn't think my father would ever forgive me if I did something to disrupt the big day.

'I'll take it to Stephen and let him decide what to do with it.'

* * *

Percy drove us to Exeter and parked on Southernhay West. It was agreed that I should go in alone, and they'd stay outside in the car.

Miss Briars regarded the grubby duffel bag suspiciously and asked me to wait while she went to check if Mr Damerell would see me.

She returned a few moments later and told me to go through to his office.

'What's that you've got there?' Stephen asked when I placed the bag on his desk.

I explained about the message we'd received from Aggy, saying she'd found Jean Claes' bag.

'No doubt you've taken a look?'

'Well, yes,' I admitted.

He grinned. 'What did you find?'

'The thing is...' I opened the bag and pointed to the notebook that was resting on top of the pile of clothes. 'He's written down Katherine's name and address.'

Stephen's grin disappeared. He picked up the notebook and was silent as he flicked through the pages.

'I wasn't sure what to do with it.'

'This chap was probably searching for a fellow countryman, and someone told him Katherine could help.' Stephen leant back in his chair, rubbing his chin. 'Leave it with me.'

I watched him closely and saw a mixture of emotions flicker across his face. I realised I'd presented him with an awkward dilemma.

'Will you take it to Superintendent Endicott?' I asked.

Before he could reply, the door was flung open and Marc burst in, breathing heavily.

'What is it?' Stephen asked. I noticed he placed the notebook on top of the clothes, pulled the bag closed, and put it on the floor behind his desk.

'It's Emile. The police have arrested him for Rupert's murder.'

27

'But why?' I gasped.

'A phial of chloral hydrate is missing from Dr Frampton's surgery. They think Emile must have taken it.' Marc paced the room, then sank into the chair by Stephen's desk.

'When did it go missing?' Stephen asked.

'The doctor noticed on Monday the sixteenth of July. He thinks it was there when he did a check the previous Monday.'

'That's a week ago,' I commented. We were all fully aware Rupert Keats was poisoned at the dinner party on Sunday the fifteenth of July, the day before Dr Frampton noticed the phial was missing.

Stephen's perplexed expression mirrored my own. 'Why didn't he report it missing sooner?'

'He didn't report it at all. He told the police when they interviewed him this morning. He said he hadn't mentioned it before because he wasn't certain how many phials there should have been.'

Stephen's brow creased. 'Why were the police interviewing Dr Frampton?'

'They wanted to know if he kept chloral hydrate at the surgery and if Emile had access to the medicine cabinet. Because he prepared the food that night, they seem to have made up their minds that he's guilty.'

Stephen sighed. 'Frampton should have reported the drug missing as soon as he knew.'

'The doctor and his wife are very fond of Emile,' I observed.

Marc turned to me accusingly. 'Of course they're fond of him. He's lived with them for five years. That doesn't mean they'd withhold information to protect him.'

I didn't reply. Stephen glanced at me. Like me, he obviously thought that was precisely what they'd done.

'Could a patient visiting the surgery have stolen it?' Stephen tried to calm the situation.

'It's in a cabinet that's kept locked. Only the doctor has the key. It's opened during the course of the day if he needs something from it. Someone could have taken it when he wasn't looking. It's unlikely to have been Emile as he's rarely there when the surgery is open.'

I couldn't help thinking it was possible Emile did know where the key to the medicine cabinet was kept. After all, he'd lodged with the Framptons for a long time. Nathalie, who'd been the doctor's receptionist during the war, would almost certainly have known. She could have told Emile. But I just couldn't picture him sneaking into the surgery in the middle of the night to steal the drug.

'Did anyone else visit the Framptons, apart from patients, during the week it's supposed to have gone missing?' I asked.

'Only dinner guests in the evening and the cabinet would be locked then,' Marc replied. 'Besides, it would have appeared odd if any guests had gone into the surgery.'

'Gwen and I had dinner with them earlier that week,' Stephen recalled. 'I think it was on Tuesday.'

'Nathalie and Annette took Timothy to have an early supper with them on the Saturday. The doctor and his wife are fond of the boy.' Marc rubbed his eyes.

'Was Emile there too?' I asked.

Marc shook his head. 'He was working and didn't get home until much later.'

Stephen picked up his pen. 'You say Frampton isn't certain a phial's missing?'

Marc shrugged. 'He says he could have been mistaken. The police don't have much to go on.'

'How is Emile?' I asked.

'Frightened.' Judging by Marc's face, Emile wasn't the only one.

Stephen regarded him for a moment, then spoke, seeming to choose his words carefully. 'I know he's your friend.' He paused. 'Can you be sure he didn't put that drug into Rupert's food?'

'I am sure.' Marc turned to me as though he expected me to back him up.

I considered the matter and decided I didn't know Emile well enough to comment. He was impetuous, and I'd occasionally seen him act rashly. However, stealing the poison days before would indicate a degree of forethought that didn't seem like Emile.

As if reading my thoughts, Marc said, 'If you're asking if Emile can sometimes be impulsive, then the answer is yes. I have known him to act unwisely. When he does, he always tells me. He swears on Nathalie and Timothy's life that he didn't poison Rupert. And I believe him.'

Stephen nodded slowly. 'What happens now?'

Marc eyed him warily. 'Superintendent Endicott has said he wants to interview everyone who was at the dinner party again.'

'Why?' Stephen asked.

'The chloral hydrate came from a distinctive green phial. He wants to know if anyone saw it that evening. Specifically, if anyone was seen handling something of that nature. And this time, he's threatening to drag everyone down to the police station.'

Stephen groaned. 'This really isn't fair on Katherine and Thomas. Not days before their wedding. And how are Bartholomew and Clementina going to feel about being taken to a police station for questioning?'

I smiled inwardly at this, knowing Nan and Gramps would enjoy the experience immensely. I could see Nan regaling her knitting circle with the tale of how she was once suspected of murder and interrogated by the police.

'If one of us had seen Emile handling a green phial, doesn't Superintendent Endicott think we would have mentioned it before now?' Stephen continued.

Marc hesitated, then said, 'I get the impression he suspects Emile may have had an accomplice and that a second person at the dinner party could have been involved in poisoning Rupert.'

I didn't say anything, but I couldn't help thinking there were only two people Emile relied upon. Nathalie and Marc. If anyone had helped him, they were the most likely candidates.

'We're being interviewed as suspects, not witnesses?' Stephen stood up. 'I think I need to pay Superintendent Endicott a visit and insist he hold any interviews here, with us in attendance.'

Marc nodded. 'I'll come with you. I want to try to see Emile.'

Feeling my presence wasn't required, I left Stephen and Marc as they prepared to visit Exeter police station. Outside in the car, I told Millicent and Percy what had happened.

'Good job Katherine hasn't booked Emile to do the catering for the wedding,' Percy remarked.

Millicent scowled. 'How can you be so callous? Emile must be terribly frightened.'

'It's not looking good.' I sighed. 'And my father and Katherine are not going to be happy when I tell them Superintendent Endicott wants to interview everyone who was at the dinner party again.'

We lapsed into silence and watched as Stephen and Marc hurried from the office.

'Where are they off to?' Percy asked.

'Waterbeer Street. Marc wants to see Emile and Stephen is going to try to persuade the superintendent to hold the interviews here again rather than at the police station.'

'What did Stephen say about Jean's bag?' Millicent asked.

'I get the impression he's not sure what to do. Then Marc came in, and I didn't want to raise the matter again.'

'It can't do any harm to leave it until after the wedding, can it?' Percy gave me a hard stare. 'Not after all this time.'

'It's not your father who's marrying...' I trailed off, my emotions conflicted. On the one hand, I didn't want to upset my father or Katherine with something that could have an entirely innocent explanation. On the other hand, I didn't want my father to discover any unpleasant truths about Katherine after he'd married her.

* * *

My heart sank when I returned to my grandparents to find Katherine seated in the parlour. Millicent hastily retreated, saying she was going upstairs to read.

Reluctantly, I sat down and told them what had happened.

'Oh no. It's only days to the wedding.' Katherine rested her head in her hands.

'I don't believe Emile had anything to do with it,' Nan said.

Katherine agreed. 'I know he and Rupert didn't get on, but I never noticed any real hate between them. Why would he do such a thing?'

But I could see my father and grandfather were beginning to have their doubts.

The only motive I could think of was that Emile wanted Nathalie and Timothy to move with him to London. I suspected Rupert Keats wouldn't have agreed to such a move. Nathalie and Annette had talked about divorce. If Rupert had refused to give Nathalie what she wanted, could Emile have decided to take care of the problem for her?

And what of the mysterious Jean Claes? Was there a link between his death and Rupert's, or were they separate incidents? That seemed like too much of a coincidence to me. The only connection I knew of between the two men was Katherine.

I thought of the way Stephen had discreetly placed Jean's bag behind his desk. I had a feeling it wouldn't be finding its way to Superintendent Endicott any time soon.

28

Superintendent Endicott decided against interviewing us in Exeter police station and allowed us to gather once again at Damerell & Tate's offices.

This time, Nathalie and Mrs Green were present. Miss Briars dealt with so many guests by arranging two rooms so Superintendent Endicott and Sergeant Hoxton could conduct the interviews concurrently.

Once again, Stephen and Marc were on hand to accompany each of us. I didn't relish another encounter with the superintendent and hoped I'd get Sergeant Hoxton. No such luck.

'I'm not sure I can tell you anything new about the dinner party,' I said.

'When we last spoke, you didn't mention that the party had moved out onto the terrace after dinner,' Superintendent Endicott replied. 'Your grandmother mentioned it, saying she'd become chilly. I'd like you to tell me in what order the guests went out and where you'd been seated before that.'

I paused, trying to picture the scene. 'I remember Mrs Jansen asking Captain Keats if we could go outside. It was a beautiful night. He went onto the terrace to light the lamps, then we all drifted out. I went first with Mrs Keats. Mrs Katherine Keats, that is. We'd been seated on the sofa nearest to the terrace doors. My father came out next with my grandparents and Mr and Mrs Damerell. They'd been on the sofas on the other side of the room.' I turned to Stephen, who'd accompanied me to the interview.

He nodded. 'Yes, I think that's my recollection.'

'What about Mr and Mrs Jansen, Mrs Nathalie Keats and Mr Vandamme?'

'They'd all been sitting at the dining table. Mr and Mrs Jansen followed Mr and Mrs Damerell out, and I think Mrs Nathalie Keats and Mr Vandamme took the opportunity to clear away a few glasses and things before joining us.'

'And Captain Keats?'

'I believe he returned to the lounge after lighting the lamps. I think it was just to get his drink because I remember him standing by the low wall of the terrace, pointing out the different landmarks along the coast. He had a brandy glass in his hand.'

'How much brandy was in it?'

I shrugged. 'I'm afraid I didn't notice.'

Superintendent Endicott turned to Stephen. 'Did you notice?'

Stephen shook his head.

'Did everyone at the party go out to the terrace?'

'Everyone except Mrs Green,' I replied. 'She remained inside.'

'The whole time?'

I frowned, trying to remember. 'I'm pretty sure she didn't join us on the terrace. I think she must have gone to the kitchen. When we returned, she'd brought out fresh pots of tea and coffee.'

After a few more questions, Superintendent Endicott seemed satisfied that I'd told him all I could remember.

He turned to Stephen. 'I'd like to speak to Mrs Jansen next. Under the circumstances, I'd prefer you to accompany her rather than her husband.'

Stephen nodded. 'I'll go and fetch her.'

We found Annette seated with my grandparents in Marc's office. Stephen explained Superintendent Endicott's request.

She regarded him with round, frightened eyes. 'Can't Marc come with me?'

'It wouldn't be appropriate under the circumstances. I'll look after you,' Stephen reassured her.

Annette nodded, but I could sense her fear. Marc seemed to share it, because after she'd left, he began to pace the room.

'How is Emile?' Nan asked.

Marc rubbed the bridge of his nose. 'Superintendent Endicott seems convinced of his guilt.' His usual assured demeanour was replaced by anxiety.

'I don't believe it,' she replied with certainty. 'I'm sure you'll prove his innocence.'

I noticed Gramps didn't comment.

'I wish I shared your faith in that.' Marc picked up a framed photograph from a shelf behind his desk. 'I couldn't bear to lose him too.'

I rose from where I'd been perching on the window sill and glanced at the photograph. It showed Marc, Emile and another young man standing close together, their arms wrapped around each other's shoulders. I remembered seeing it before. It was the photograph Marc and Emile had shown to new arrivals at Park Fever Hospital when they were searching for news of their friend.

'Did you find him?' I nodded at the photograph and pointed to the grainy image of a dark-haired young man who wore a defiant expression.

'He was Annette's brother,' Marc said softly. 'He was killed.'

'I'm sorry.'

'Shot by the Germans. He was part of a resistance group responsible for the demolition of bridges and railway lines. The Germans retaliated.'

'How did you find out?'

'Katherine told us.'

'Katherine?' I experienced a feeling of apprehension. Why did everything keep coming back to her?

'After we left the hospital and came here, we gave her a copy of this photograph, and she asked around for us to see if anyone knew what had become of Ferdinand Peeters.'

I was beginning to realise the extent of the work Katherine had done in collating information from the thousands of refugees she'd come into contact with. Stephen was right. Someone could have given her name to Jean Claes and told him she might be able to help him find whoever he was searching for.

Gramps came over to gaze at the photograph. 'You all look as though you're about to take on the world.'

Marc smiled. 'My father took it just before Ferdinand and I went away to university to study law. Emile was already training as a chef.'

'Ferdinand.' Nan pronounced each syllable. 'That's a lovely, strong name.'

I stared at the picture wondering where I'd heard the name recently. I couldn't discern much of a resemblance between the tall man in the photograph and the petite Annette, apart from the thick dark hair.

'It means daring, brave. It was true of him. The bravest of us all.' Marc smiled sadly. 'I couldn't bear to lose Emile too.'

Nan squeezed Marc's arm. 'It won't come to that. The truth will prevail.'

Marc put his arm around her and gave her a hug. 'Thank you for your belief.'

I hoped she was right. But what was the truth?

I left Damerell & Tate's offices with my grandparents and told them I was going to meet Percy and Millicent at Dellers for lunch.

I found them seated at a table on the second-floor balcony. They'd been keen to experience the opulent café for themselves. Percy's legs were jerking along to the music of the orchestra below.

'Well?' Millicent asked eagerly.

I told them Superintendent Endicott had been interested in where everyone was sitting after dinner and in which order we'd gone out to the terrace. 'I guess he thinks that's when it happened.'

'If that's the case, then surely it's less likely to be Emile,' Millicent commented. 'The chloral hydrate must have been administered in Rupert's drink rather than the food. Anyone could have done it.'

I thought about this. It was true. With planning, anyone in the room could have contrived to have slipped the poison into Rupert's brandy.

'Who are the most likely suspects?' Percy asked.

'Rupert went out to the terrace to light the lamps. If it happened at that point, I was chatting with Katherine, and my father and grandparents were with Stephen and Gwen, which means none of them could have done it.'

'Which leaves' – Percy paused dramatically – 'Emile, Nathalie, Marc and Annette.'

'And Mrs Green,' Millicent added.

He wrinkled his nose. 'You suspect the housekeeper? I suppose there are the dodgy goings on over the will.'

I shrugged. 'She's supposed to be devoted to the Keats family. I'm not sure she'd do anything to harm one of them.'

'Suppose she realised Rupert had deceived her over the major's will,' Millicent suggested. 'She could have wanted revenge?'

Percy and I didn't think much of that idea. We continued to concoct different theories while tucking into a lunch of crab meat sandwiches followed by Devonshire tea and freshly baked scones with cream and jam.

After lunch, we went to explore Exeter Cathedral. Apart from the first weekend when we'd toured Dartmoor, we'd done little sightseeing on our holiday. Instead, we'd spent most of our time investigating the mystery of the man in the cave. I was conscious of the fact that we'd be leaving Devon in six days' time, and the case hadn't been solved. Although we knew the identity of the man, we still didn't know how he'd died or why he'd ended up in Smugglers Cove.

We whiled away the remainder of the afternoon strolling around Exeter before Percy drove back to Dawlish and Millicent and I returned to my grandparents.

'You're quiet,' Millicent observed when we reached Bedford Circus. 'What are you worrying about?'

'I'm confused,' I replied.

She gave me a searching look. 'About Jean Claes, Rupert Keats or your father's marriage?'

I smiled. 'All three.'

'Do you want to talk about it?'

I shook my head. 'I'm too muddled to explain. I'd like to go for a walk to think about things.'

She took the hint. 'I'll tell your grandparents you had some last-minute shopping to do before the wedding, and you'll be back in time for dinner.'

'Thank you.'

Before she opened the front door, she said, 'For what it's worth, I think Katherine is a decent woman.'

I nodded and walked away slowly. If Millicent was watching, I wanted it to appear as though I had no particular destination in mind. In truth, I knew exactly where I was going.

When I reached the Higher Cemetery, I went to the grave where Jean Claes was buried. The flowers that had been left in the glass jar by the wooden cross had wilted. I bent down to pick up one of the drooping roses. The pink petals had turned brown, and the strong fruity fragrance was gone.

'Hello. You back again?'

I looked up to find the old groundsman leaning against his handcart, watching me.

I pointed to the flowers. 'Last time I was here, you told me that a dark-haired woman had brought these roses. Was she an older lady?'

He shook his head. 'Not old. A pretty young thing. Big brown eyes and short dark hair.'

After he'd wandered away, pushing his handcart, I went to sit on a bench under a nearby yew tree.

It was the perfect place to reflect on all that had happened in the past weeks. The peace of the cemetery helped me to clear my head and focus on the facts. Our holiday certainly hadn't turned out as I'd imagined. Sadly, I was now convinced our discovery at Smugglers Cove on that first day had led to Captain Keats' death.

I'd assumed Mrs Green had taken the roses from the garden at Smugglers Haunt and put them on her nephew's grave. But it wasn't Arnold in the grave, and it hadn't been Mrs Green who'd brought the flowers. I was certain I knew who'd placed those roses by the wooden cross.

Half an hour later, I was proved right. The petite figure of

Annette Jansen came into view. She didn't notice me under the yew tree.

I watched as she removed the wilted roses from the glass jar. She stood for a few minutes, dabbing her eyes with a handkerchief. Then she muttered some words before making the sign of the cross and walking away, clutching the dead flowers.

I thought back to when Nathalie had shown me the roses growing in the garden of Smugglers Haunt. She'd said they were a new variety from France given to her by her godmother. A new breed of rose called Ferdinand Pichard.

* * *

It was six o'clock by the time I left the cemetery and arrived back at Damerell & Tate's offices. Miss Briars wasn't happy to see me.

'I'm afraid both Mr Damerell and Mr Jansen have left for the day.' She smiled politely but glanced at her watch, clearly wanting to leave herself.

'I'm not here to see them. I left my gloves in Mr Jansen's office earlier today. Would you mind if I popped in and grabbed them?'

'I suppose that would be alright.' She went to get up, but I sailed past her desk.

I dashed into the office, grabbed the framed photograph of Marc, Emile and Ferdinand from the shelf and shoved it in my bag. I pulled my gloves out of my pocket as the receptionist reached the door.

'Here they are.' I waved them at her. 'Thank you so much.'

29

The following morning, Millicent and I hopped on the train once more. But when it stopped at Dawlish, I didn't get off. Millicent jumped down onto the platform and turned to find I was still on the train.

'I need to see Aggy again,' I called as the train pulled out.

I felt guilty when I saw the confusion on her face. I'd considered telling her what I suspected – then decided I needed to check whether I was right or not before I confided in anyone. No doubt Percy would be annoyed with me.

From the window, I watched the holidaymakers on the seafront before the carriage was plunged into the darkness of Kennaway Tunnel. The train emerged briefly into daylight at Coryton Cove before entering Coryton Tunnel. When it came out above Smugglers Cove, I studied the beach below with interest.

Although anyone on the train would have a clear view of the beach, they wouldn't be able to see the foot of the cliffs or the cave. The slope down from Smugglers Haunt ran over the top of the tunnel, so only the lower section could be seen briefly as the train sped by before entering Phillot Tunnel.

When I got to Teignmouth, I went to the ticket office to pay the additional fare, then strolled through the town to the seafront and Den Crescent.

Rita answered the door of the Pier View boarding house.

'Hello. Mum was just talking about you. Come in, she's in the kitchen. She's dying to know if you've discovered anything about that poor man.'

I followed Rita to the kitchen at the back of the house, where Aggy was elbow deep in soapy water, washing up the breakfast things.

She picked up a tea towel and dried her hands. 'Sit down, the tea in that pot's still warm, or I can make you a fresh one?'

I took the cup she offered and said warm tea was fine.

We sat at the table and she refilled her cup. 'Have you found out anything about Jean?'

'Maybe.' I reached into my bag, pulled out the photograph I'd taken from Marc's office, and handed it to her.

She studied it, then pointed to Ferdinand Peeters. 'That's Jean. Not that he looked like that when he stayed here. He was much thinner and older. But it's definitely the same man.'

Rita peered over her shoulder. 'Yes. That's him.'

Aggy regarded me expectantly. 'Have you found his family?'

I nodded. 'I've found his sister.'

* * *

I took the train back to Dawlish and made my way up Bere Hill to Primrose Lodge.

I was glad to find Katherine was alone. Gwen had taken Bea and Charlie shopping in Exeter and Stephen was at work. We went into the garden and Bruno ambled over to greet me.

I took the photograph out of my bag and handed it to Katherine. 'Have you seen this picture before?'

She took it and gazed at it in surprise. 'I remember Marc and Emile showing me this when they came here in the summer of 1917. They were trying to find out if anyone had heard anything of Annette's brother. I'm afraid it wasn't good news.'

I fondled Bruno's ears and he flopped down at my feet. 'What happened to him?'

'He was a member of the resistance. As were Emile and Marc. They were smuggled out of the country when things got too dangerous but Ferdinand Peeters got left behind. I heard from more than one source that he'd been shot. The Germans knew Ferdinand was part of a resistance unit based in Flanders that were extremely efficient at blowing up bridges and railway lines. The unit seemed to have a knack of breaking through any weakness in the German defence.'

'When did you learn of his death?'

She paused to consider. 'It was later in 1917, I think in September or October. I remember Emile and Marc had already joined up. I had to tell Annette.' Her eyes grew misty at the memory.

'I showed this photograph to Aggy Challacombe. She's the lady that runs the boarding house where Jean Claes was staying when he disappeared.' I pointed to Ferdinand. 'This is Jean Claes.'

The shock and confusion on Katherine's face seemed genuine. If she was faking it, she was a better actress than Dame Cicely. 'You mean it was Ferdinand Peeters' body in the cave?'

I nodded. 'Do you know why he might have changed his name?'

Her brow creased as she thought about this. Slowly, she said, 'If Jean Claes was Ferdinand Peeters, it's likely he instigated the story of his own death. He probably had no choice but to adopt a new identity. It would have been too dangerous for him to have been caught with anything that could identify him. He'd have had to destroy any documents that showed his real name.'

'You think he would have been shot if he'd been captured?'

She paused. 'He would have been tortured for information first. They'd have pressured him to give up the names of his accomplices.'

I felt sick. 'So he became Jean Claes?'

'It seems likely. Annette Jansen was his only living relative, and she was safely over here. There was an uncle who died shortly before Emile and Marc escaped. They told me he'd been shot. The Germans believed he was helping Ferdinand. It's probably the reason Ferdinand decided to fake his own death. Anyone who knew him would have been in danger.'

'What would he do after the war if he had no documents in his real name?'

'I assume he came to England to find Annette and Marc. With their help, he'd be able to prove who he was.' She'd been staring sadly at the photograph. Now her head shot up, and she gave me a penetrating look. 'You think he went to Smugglers Haunt in search of me?'

'When she first arrived in England, Nathalie got word to Emile that she and Annette were being put on one of the trains transporting refugees to Devon. Emile would have told Ferdinand.'

'So he came to Devon in search of them? And you think someone told him I'd be able to help him to locate where they were living?'

I nodded.

Tears filled her eyes. 'I don't understand how he ended up in the cave at Smugglers Cove. Was I somehow responsible?'

'No. Sadly you weren't there when Ferdinand knocked on the door of Smugglers Haunt,' I replied softly. 'And he had no idea of what he was walking into.'

Comprehension dawned, and I saw dismay in her eyes. 'Rupert?'

'Before she and Annette left Belgium, Nathalie became secretly engaged to Ferdinand. When Rupert first proposed to Nathalie, she told him she couldn't marry him as she was promised to Annette's brother.'

Katherine breathed heavily, raising her hand to her mouth in horror. 'How would Rupert have known who he was?'

'Ferdinand must have told him who he was trying to find. And why.'

She let out a low moan. 'It's even possible Rupert recognised him. I had a copy of this photograph, and so did Nathalie and Annette. He could have seen it at some point.'

Katherine was silent for a moment, gently touching the face of the young man in the photograph. Then she said, 'Do you really believe Rupert killed him?'

I nodded.

She brushed away a tear. 'And Emile discovered the truth?'

I stroked Bruno's head as I considered this. 'No,' I said eventually. 'I don't think so.'

Her eyes widened. 'I don't understand. Who was responsible for Rupert's death?'

'I'm not certain,' I replied. But as I said it, I began to connect the series of events that had led to Rupert being poisoned. 'In a way, I think I might have been.'

30

After promising Katherine I'd tell Stephen everything I'd learnt, I caught a train back to Exeter.

When I arrived at Damerell & Tate's, I wondered how I was going to sneak the photograph back into Marc's office. With any luck, he might not have noticed it was missing. This was probably wishful thinking on my part, and I knew I had to prepare myself for a difficult conversation.

It turned out to be easier than expected. Miss Briars told me that both Stephen and Marc were at Exeter police station.

'Has something happened?' I hoped the police hadn't yet charged Emile.

'I'm afraid I can't say,' Miss Briars replied primly.

'Would you mind if I went to Mr Damerell's office and left a note?'

She sighed, waving a hand. 'You know where it is.'

I thanked her and quickly walked along the corridor. First, I went into Marc's office and replaced the photograph on the shelf. Then I went across the hall into Stephen's office and sat at his desk.

Jean Claes' bag was still on the floor. I didn't blame Stephen for not wanting to stir up more trouble for Katherine. It was Wednesday, and the wedding was on Saturday. By the expression on Katherine's face when I'd left, she was scared something else was going to happen before the big day.

I picked up a pen, then put it down again. Leaning back in the chair, I realised there was nothing I could write in a note. Mainly because I wasn't sure if my suspicion was correct – and even if it was, I had little way of proving it.

I rocked back and forth in the chair for a few moments, aware I'd have to move soon or Miss Briars would come to see what I was up to. Eventually, I got up, left the office, said goodbye to Miss Briars and wandered into the town centre.

I was tempted to go to the police station to see what was happening. However, I knew that no one, least of all Superintendent Endicott, was likely to welcome my presence.

Instead, I called in at a bakery by the cathedral and bought a Devonshire pasty. Then I returned to the Higher Cemetery, sat on the bench by the yew tree, and prepared myself for a long and possibly pointless wait. It was probably a futile exercise but I had a strong suspicion that the glass jar wouldn't remain empty for long. Annette, or someone else, would come and put fresh flowers on Ferdinand's grave.

I'd seen enough of Annette to know she wouldn't be able to keep something like this to herself. Or act on her own. She relied on two people. Nathalie and Marc.

I took out the pasty and sat nibbling it from its paper bag, sharing crumbs with a flock of sparrows. The afternoon wore on, and I had to acknowledge that with only five days left in Devon, it was unlikely I'd discover the whole truth before I had to return home. I'd have to put all the evidence I'd found in Stephen's hands and leave him to do what he could with it.

I decided to go back to Damerell & Tate's before Stephen went home for the day. I stood up, brushed the crumbs from my skirt, went over to the rubbish bin and threw away the paper bag. I was about to leave the cemetery when I spotted a figure approaching Ferdinand Peeters' grave.

I let out a long breath. It was who I'd been expecting.

Nathalie Keats knelt down and placed a handful of the magenta-striped roses into the glass jar. Her blonde hair fell across her face, and she raised a hand to push it back and brush away a tear.

I took a few steps towards the grave. Then, to my confusion, I realised someone else was watching Nathalie. They'd followed her into the cemetery at a discreet distance.

It was Marc.

31

Marc and I saw each other at the same moment. We both stopped, momentarily at a loss as to what to do next.

Nathalie was kneeling by the grave, oblivious to our presence. It was a strange triangle. Marc stared at me in confusion. I looked back at him, doubts rising in my mind.

Why was he here?

In the same moment, we moved towards Nathalie. She saw Marc first and then me. Initially startled, she quickly composed herself.

She touched the simple wooden cross that marked the grave and murmured something – then stood up to face us.

Marc studied the grave as if willing it to yield its secrets. 'You believe the body found in the cave was Ferdinand, don't you?' he asked, his voice hoarse with emotion. 'Why?'

Nathalie turned to me. 'You described his ring to Mrs Green.'

I bit my lip. If I'd kept my mouth shut, Rupert Keats might still be alive.

Nathalie's fingers went to her throat, and she held up a ring that hung from a chain around her neck. It was identical to the one I'd seen on the skeletal finger of the man in the cave. A solid silver band engraved with tiny doves.

'We had them made secretly. We wanted to marry, but my parents wouldn't allow it. They said Ferdinand and I had to wait until after the war when things were more settled. Before we parted, we exchanged rings. Doves to symbolise our love and our hope for peace. No one knew, not even Emile.'

'Not even Annette?' I asked. When I'd described the ring to Mrs Green, both Nathalie and Annette had been in earshot.

'No. She never knew,' Nathalie said vehemently. A little too vehemently. I didn't believe her. I was certain she would have confided her secret engagement to her closest friend, Ferdinand's sister.

Marc's face was pale and I was convinced he shared that suspicion. I guessed it was why he'd followed Nathalie to the cemetery. He knew as well as I did that Annette would jump at Nathalie's every command.

'You've been bringing these roses to his grave?' Marc pointed to the glass jar.

She nodded.

Nathalie wasn't the petite dark-haired woman the groundsman had described. I studied Marc's bewildered face. 'Is that what made you think something was wrong?'

He nodded. 'When I came to find you that day to tell you Rupert had been poisoned, I noticed them. I recognised them as the Ferdinand Pichard variety that Nathalie's godmother had given her. I assumed at the time Mrs Green must have brought them, though I thought it odd she would have taken those particular roses. She knew how Nathalie treasured them. When Arnold Rowe turned up alive, it made me wonder even more.'

'A Ferdinand rose for your fiancé, Ferdinand,' I said to Nathalie.

'My godmother knew what he'd meant to me and gave me the rose as a way of remembering him. I didn't have a grave to visit, but I had my bold, dramatic flowers.' She regarded me coldly. 'I don't understand how you guessed.'

'Marc showed my grandparents and me the photograph of him with Ferdinand and Emile. Ferdinand isn't a common name in this country yet I knew I'd heard it recently. Then I remembered it was the name of the unusual rose in your garden. I thought it a strange coincidence those roses should have been placed on the grave of Arnold Rowe.'

'Did you take my photograph?' Marc asked.

'I wanted to know for sure. I took it to show Aggy Challacombe, the landlady of the Pier View boarding house. She recognised Ferdinand as her lodger, Jean Claes.'

Marc rubbed his bleary eyes. 'I don't understand. Why was he at Smugglers Cove? What happened to him?'

'Rupert,' I said softly.

Nathalie made a noise like a cat hissing.

Marc stared at her. 'Did he? Rupert, did he...?'

She nodded.

'Why?'

Her lips trembled. 'Because of me. Rupert had dreamt for so long of us marrying and living at Smugglers Haunt.'

'And then your fiancé turned up, back from the dead?' The words felt heavy with the knowledge of how brief his return to life had been.

'That night, after I heard you talking to Mrs Green about the ring, I got Rupert drunk. I goaded him into telling me what happened. He tried to deny it.' Nathalie spat with disgust. 'But I knew. From the moment I heard you describe a silver ring engraved with doves, I knew.'

'How did Rupert know who Jean Claes was?' I asked.

'When he came to Smugglers Haunt looking for Katherine, Rupert invited him in. They chatted and Ferdinand told him he was searching for his sister and fiancée. He gave Rupert our names.'

And his fate was sealed. It was so heartbreakingly sad after all Ferdinand had endured.

'Rupert killed him?' Pain and anger distorted Marc's handsome features.

'He claims it was an accident,' Nathalie sneered. 'That he panicked. He gave Ferdinand a glass of whisky and put chloral hydrate in it. It was a drug prescribed to Laurence to help him sleep. Katherine was due back, and he wanted to stop Ferdinand from speaking to her. She would have reunited him with Annette and me. Rupert said he put the drug in his drink to knock him out.' Her pale blue eyes turned liquid with tears. 'But Ferdinand was thin and not in good health. He didn't survive. Rupert dragged his body down to the beach and hid him in the cave.'

Marc covered his face with his hands and began to sob. In that moment, any lingering suspicion that it might have been him who had aided Nathalie disappeared. His shock and distress were real.

I reached out my hand to comfort him, but Nathalie got there first. She enveloped him in a tight embrace. 'I'm sorry, Marc.'

'Ferdinand wasn't dead?' His voice was little more than a whisper. 'All that time? Why did Katherine tell us he was?'

'Because that's what she'd been told by more than one source.' I repeated what Katherine had said to me. 'She thinks he instigated the story of his own death and took on the identity of Jean Claes to protect himself and others. His uncle had already been shot by the Germans in their search for Ferdinand.'

'He survived and came to find us.' Marc sobbed into Nathalie's shoulder.

'That is why I had to make Rupert pay,' she hissed into his ear, holding him close.

Marc released himself from her grasp. 'You poisoned Rupert?' He brushed the tears from his face with the sleeve of his jacket.

'I knew he would drink too much at the party. But he always managed to stay the upright gentleman. The good captain, who got his commission because of his family connections rather than his bravery. I wanted him to be...' She screwed up her face trying to find the right words. '...falling down drunk. So I drugged his brandy.'

I remembered Katherine saying how Rupert 'always stayed just the right side of drunk'.

'He did more than fall down, Nathalie,' Marc retorted angrily.

'Don't you hate him for what he did?' she spat.

'Of course I do,' he growled. 'But—'

'I wanted to humiliate him. No.' She shook her head and corrected herself. 'I wanted him to humiliate himself. In front of people. Witnesses.'

Marc stared at her. 'Did you mean to kill him?'

'I wanted to punish him for what he did. My life with him is not the life I should have had. It's not even the life he promised me. I'd already planned to divorce him and go with you and Annette to London. Emile said he would support Timothy and me.'

Marc gripped her arm. 'Does Emile know? Did he help you?'

'Of course not. He would have done something foolish if he'd found out.' She stopped, realising what she'd said, then waved her hand in a gesture of resignation. 'Yes. What I did was foolish. All of it. I was stupid to have ever married Rupert. I never loved him. But I thought my fiancé was dead, so it didn't matter who I married.'

'When you poured chloral hydrate into his drink, did you think Rupert would die?' Marc demanded.

'I knew it was a possibility.' She shrugged as though it were a matter of indifference to her. 'He deserved it. After all Ferdinand had been through. To die like that. Our beloved Ferdinand.'

Marc shed more tears, this time silently.

'You used chloral hydrate? The same drug he gave Ferdinand?' I wanted to hear every detail because I still wasn't convinced she'd acted alone.

'I gave him the same odds as he gave Ferdinand,' she snarled.

'Why didn't you tell the police what Rupert had done? Instead of taking matters into your own hands?'

She shrugged. 'I did it for Ferdinand.'

'It's not what he would have wanted,' Marc said softly.

'I told you about the ring on Friday the thirteenth of July. The following evening, when you had supper with the Framptons, you stole the phial of chloral hydrate.'

Nathalie touched the handbag which rested on her arm. 'The empty phial is in here. Emile didn't take it. He wouldn't have a clue where to look. I knew where Dr Frampton kept the key to the medicine cabinet. I made an excuse to go to the bathroom during supper and went into the surgery. I only took one phial of chloral hydrate. I hoped it wouldn't be missed.'

One phial was all it had taken to kill her husband. 'Did Annette create a diversion for you so you wouldn't be missed by the Framptons?'

'Iris. Please.' Marc stared at me pleadingly. 'Don't say any more, Nathalie. We need to talk about this.'

'At the dinner party on Sunday night, you were able to pour the drug into Rupert's brandy without being seen. Did you do it after Annette had got us all out onto the terrace?' My implication was clear.

'I've already told you.' Nathalie jabbed at my chest ferociously. 'Annette does not know about this.'

I held my ground. 'Then why has she been coming here putting roses on her brother's grave?'

'I gave her the roses and asked her to put them on the grave. I told her they were from Mrs Green for her nephew.' Nathalie backed away from me and spoke in a more conciliatory tone. 'Annette is not involved. And neither is Emile. I was wrong to do what I did, and I regret it. I came to say goodbye to Ferdinand before going to the police.'

'You're going to confess?' Marc's expression showed relief and alarm.

She nodded, seeming unperturbed. 'That's why I have the empty phial in my handbag. I'd like you to come with me to the police station. Do you think I could speak with Emile before seeing Superintendent Endicott?'

Marc didn't answer. His eyes locked with mine.

'Take me to the police station,' Nathalie said impatiently. 'I want to see Emile.'

He shook his head. 'First, you need to come back to the office with me. We have to discuss what you're going to say. Then I'll talk to Stephen. It will be best if he goes with you to see Superintendent Endicott. I'll carry on representing Emile.' Marc may have been talking to Nathalie but his eyes didn't leave my face.

I guessed he was waiting to see how I'd react. I stayed silent.

Nathalie looked from him to me and then nodded. 'If you think that would be best.'

Without a word, I turned and walked towards the cemetery gates. Superintendent Endicott could make what he wanted of their story. I'd found out what I needed to know. My involvement was over.

32

'Please, no further revelations,' Katherine begged when Percy, Millicent and I turned up at Primrose Lodge the day before the wedding.

'None whatsoever. We're going to be on our best behaviour from now on, I promise.' Percy produced a bouquet of flowers from behind his back and handed them to her.

'How lovely!' Katherine exclaimed in surprise.

Lizzy, our housekeeper, appeared and wrapped her arms around me. 'You can't keep out of trouble, can you?'

I distracted her by asking, 'How was your journey down?'

'I'm never getting in a car with that woman ever again.' Lizzy shuddered with what seemed like genuine fear.

She had my sympathy. Mrs Siddons' confidence as a driver wasn't matched by her ability behind the wheel. 'How are you going to get home?'

'I'll catch the train.'

Millicent gave Katherine an embroidered chimney sweep. 'We wanted to thank you for inviting us and wish you luck. My pupils helped me make it. In case a chimney sweep doesn't make an appearance on the day.'

Katherine laughed. 'How fortunate. I haven't included a chimney sweep on the guest list, although I'm aware of the tradition. I'm sure this will do just as well.'

I handed her a small, framed watercolour I'd picked up in a gallery close to Exeter Cathedral. It was a charming picture of Coryton Cove. 'To remind you of the sea when you're living in Walden,' I said. 'We only have a lake.'

'It's beautiful.' She hugged me and I returned the embrace. 'A lake is fine by me. I'm looking forward to us living there together.'

'Me too.' Though not in the same house, I mentally added.

They went out into the garden, Millicent explaining to a bemused Bea and Charlie that chimney sweeps were supposed to bring the bride good luck.

I was about to follow when Stephen beckoned me into his study. I sat by his desk, bracing myself for the conversation to follow.

'Marc said that when you and he spoke to Nathalie in the cemetery, she was already planning to go to the police. Is that true?'

'Yes. She had the empty chloral hydrate phial in her handbag. She wouldn't have let Emile take the blame.'

He seemed to relax. 'Good. That's what Marc said. I wanted to hear it from you too. If I'm to represent Nathalie, I needed to be sure she hadn't been forced to do it. Hopefully, her voluntary confession will go in her favour.'

'Has Emile been released?'

He nodded. 'Chap's in a terrible state. He didn't have a clue what was going on. Marc and Annette are looking after him and Timothy. I'll do what I can for Nathalie. God knows, I can see how she was driven to it. She told me what Rupert did. She only wanted him to fall down drunk; she never meant for him to die. I think a jury will see that.'

Marc had evidently guided Nathalie on the best line to take in order to help Stephen defend her prosecution. It was also clear that no mention would be made of Annette's possible involvement. I was certain she'd helped Nathalie, though I was less sure if she'd been aware of how dangerous chloral hydrate could be.

For Timothy's sake, I hoped the jury would be lenient on Nathalie. The poor child had already lost his father. He was no doubt wondering where his mother had gone. I was glad he had Emile, Marc and Annette to care for him.

Stephen suddenly pushed his chair back and stood up, surprising Bruno, who'd been resting on his lap. 'Sorry, old boy.' He ruffled the dog's ears absentmindedly, his thoughts clearly elsewhere. 'The problem is, there's no proof that Rupert killed Ferdinand Peeters. Without it, Nathalie's defence will be weak. There's nothing to corroborate her story.'

'There could be someone who might be able to help.'

'Who?'

'Harriet Green.'

Stephen considered this. He went over to the window and peered out to the garden. 'Come with me to Smugglers Haunt.'

'Now?' I said, mindful of the fact we'd just promised Katherine there would be no further revelations.

'Yes. Let's go while everyone's occupied. I need to resolve this once and for all.'

Bruno was pushed out of the way as a determined Stephen strode from the room. I jumped up and followed. Outside, I could see Percy and Millicent playing tennis with Bea and Charlie. Katherine, Lizzy and Gwen were watching. We slipped into Stephen's car and drove away unnoticed.

I stood at his side as he rapped on the door of Smugglers

Haunt, beginning to regret what I'd said about Mrs Green. It was entirely possible I'd got this all wrong.

Harriet Green opened the door and without a word, stepped aside to let us in. She seemed to have aged since I last saw her. Her black hair hadn't been dyed recently and grey roots were showing. The creases around her eyes and mouth seemed to have grown deeper.

We followed her into the lounge, where I went over to the window and looked down at Smugglers Cove to the cave where Ferdinand Peeters had been concealed for five years.

Mrs Green joined me by the window. 'I didn't know who he was.'

'But you knew it wasn't your nephew.' Stephen gestured for her to sit down.

She took a seat on one of the sofas, her hands folded in front of her. Stephen and I sat on the sofa across from her, watching her expression change as she told us about the day Ferdinand called at Smugglers Haunt.

'I wasn't here when he arrived. I'd been shopping in town. When I got back it was too late.' She pointed at the carpet by the terrace doors. 'He was lying dead on the floor.'

Stephen breathed heavily. 'Captain Keats killed him?'

'It was an accident. He'd put a drug in his drink – he must have used too much.'

'Why on earth didn't you call the police?' Stephen demanded.

'It wouldn't have been fair for Captain Keats to get in trouble for protecting his brother. He told me the man was German and that he'd tried to kill Major Keats. The Germans needed to make sure the major died so he couldn't testify to the atrocities he'd witnessed in Belgium and France.'

'And you believed him?' Stephen asked incredulously.

'I did at the time. I knew Major Keats had been involved with the intelligence corps. It must have been true.' She looked at him desperately. 'Why else would Captain Keats have drugged the man?'

'The man's real name was Ferdinand Peeters. He was Annette Jansen's brother. And Nathalie's fiancé.' I saw her expression change.

Harriet Green's head dropped into her hands and she began to weep. We watched her in silence. Eventually, she lifted her head. 'When the body was found, I... I began to doubt the story. I didn't know what to think. Why would Captain Keats have done such a thing?'

'Presumably for the same reason he decided to add a fraudulent codicil to his brother's will,' Stephen said dryly.

'Rupert had a dream that I think became an obsession,' I explained. 'He dreamt of marrying Nathalie Vandamme and living with her here in Smugglers Haunt, his family home. That was why he changed his brother's will. And it was why he ended up killing Ferdinand Peeters.'

'If I'd known, I'd never have...' She sobbed and covered her face with her hands.

'You'd never have helped him move the body to the cave?' I suggested.

She gave a series of gasps as though she couldn't inhale enough air.

Stephen stared at her, shaking his head in disbelief. 'I can understand your loyalty to Laurence. He was a good man. But Rupert? Why did you pretend you'd witnessed Laurence signing the codicil to his will when you hadn't? And persuaded your nephew to do the same?'

She raised her chin defiantly. 'Because Smugglers Haunt should stay in the Keats family.'

'Katherine was Major Keats' wife,' he protested.

'I know she loved him. But she ought to have stayed with him day and night. He was dying. She had no right to keep going up to London like she did.'

I tried to push thoughts of when Katherine's relationship with my father had started from my mind. As Percy said, what did it matter? But it did matter. Had Katherine been meeting my father in London when her husband was dying?

'She didn't have a choice. She was involved in essential war work,' Stephen said through gritted teeth.

'I won't deny she was extremely kind to those refugees. No one could have worked harder. But she should have put her husband first. Not worried about finding bed and board for strangers.'

'She did more than that,' Stephen spluttered.

I could feel his rage simmering below the surface. And I wanted to know why.

'What did she do that was so important?' I asked. 'Why did she leave her dying husband? The war was over.'

My provocation worked.

'She risked her life for her country, that's what,' he shouted. 'Katherine did more than interview refugees. She was in the intelligence corps too. They sent her into occupied territory.'

Mrs Green's mouth dropped open. So did mine.

'She... she was a spy?' I stammered.

'She was given false papers and sent into occupied Belgium on more than one occasion. If they'd captured her, she would have been tortured and shot.' Stephen took a deep breath, trying to control his fury, which was clearly born of frustration at having to keep this secret for so long. 'She didn't want to leave Laurence, but she had no say in the matter. They kept calling her in to verify accounts of what she'd witnessed in Belgium and sign statements. They tried to make it as easy for her as they could, but on occasion, they needed to interview her in person.'

'I didn't know,' Mrs Green muttered.

'Now you do.' Stephen's anger still simmered. 'She went through unimaginable horror. And when the war ended, she lost her husband and her home. You have no idea how much she suffered. I intend to contest Laurence's will. This house should be Katherine's. And when she gets it, I doubt she'll want you in it.'

Mrs Green wiped her eyes with a handkerchief and then placed it in the pocket of her apron. 'I know I can't stay here. I've already made plans to go and live with my brother.' She folded her hands on her lap and said calmly, 'I'm sorry for what I did. I can only say I did it with the best of intentions. Over the years, it's weighed heavily on me. Now I know the truth, I'll be glad to tell the police everything and accept whatever punishment comes my way.' She stood up. 'I'm going to do it today.'

'My car's outside. I'll drive you to Exeter police station.' Stephen's anger seemed to have abated. 'If you wish, I'll ask Superintendent Endicott if I can be present when you're interviewed.'

She nodded. 'Thank you. You're very kind. It's more than I deserve.' She untied the apron from around her waist. 'I'll fetch my coat and bag.'

I waited for her to leave the room before asking, 'Is that how Katherine met my father?'

Stephen hesitated, then his shoulders sagged. 'What does it matter now? I can't tell you too much. I don't actually know all of the operations she was involved in. She was sent in to gather intelligence from locals about German troop movements. She reported to liaison officers at the Dutch border. I believe your father and Elijah were helping to channel the information she received to some of their news agency contacts.'

I stayed silent, letting this sink in.

'You've been suspicious of her, haven't you?' he said bluntly.

'I know when I'm being lied to,' I retorted.

He held out his hands. 'They had no choice.'

'I understand that now.'

He regarded me curiously. 'Does this mean the marriage has your blessing?'

The following day, my father would be marrying a spy. Not a murderer. Or an adulteress.

I nodded.

33

'I say, Millicent.' Percy stood back and stared blatantly at Millicent's ankles. He'd been waiting for us by the lychgate of St Michael's and All Angels church.

She blushed a deep crimson. 'I'm not sure what my pupils would make of me dressed like this.' When we were getting ready, she'd confessed to never having worn a calf-length frock before. 'Ursula made me buy it.'

'You look absolutely ravishing. If Daniel could see you now...'

Percy's friend, Daniel Timpson, owner of Crookham Hall, was known to be smitten with Millicent. So far, she'd kept him at arm's length. But I had a feeling that buying a calf-length dress was the start of a whole new world for Miss Millicent Nightingale, though she'd refused my offer to dust her face with powder and apply a little rouge.

Percy stood back to examine me, and I gave a twirl in the pale blue dress, cream shoes and cloche hat that Katherine had bought for me.

'You look jolly pretty, too,' he said with a wink.

'You cut quite a dash yourself.' I winked back. He did look

smart, though there was something different about him that I couldn't quite place.

'Oh, this old thing.' Percy gestured to what was obviously a new pale grey flannel morning suit with matching waistcoat. He'd finished it off with a grey fedora hat and a narrow pink tie.

'You've shaved your moustache off!' Millicent exclaimed.

'I know you hated it,' he said with a sacrificial air.

'Much better.' I smiled, not daring to admit I hadn't immediately noticed it had gone.

My grandparents came up at that moment and Nan clapped her hands together. 'Percy! So handsome. I hope you'll be able to tear yourself away from these pretty young things to dance with this old lady at the reception.'

My grandmother had enjoyed getting dressed up as much as Millicent and I had. She'd joined us in our bedroom and liberally sprayed herself with my perfume before dusting herself with my powder and applying some of my lip colour.

'Try and stop me, Clementina. Do you know the foxtrot?'

'No, but I'm not too old to learn. What about you, dear?' she asked my grandfather.

'Not on your life,' Gramps replied. 'Perhaps Millicent would care to join me for an old-fashioned waltz?'

Millicent smiled. 'I'd be delighted.'

Gramps took Nan's hand and they strolled over to where Bea and Charlie Damerell were handing out the order of service.

Percy insisted on linking arms with both Millicent and me and escorting us into the church. It was a hot afternoon, and the ancient building was blissfully cool inside.

I felt a flutter of emotion when I saw my father standing by the altar in a slim-fitting navy flannel morning suit. Katherine wore a beautifully cut dove-grey dress and carried a small bouquet of pale pink roses. They made an attractive couple.

Elijah stood by my father's side, splendid in a traditional grey morning suit with pin-striped trousers and a red Ascot cravat. I was sure Horace was responsible for the expert tying of the cravat, and the neat placement of the red pocket handkerchief and red rose buttonhole.

After all the preparations, I'd expected a long waffling service. But what followed was a simple, and – I had to admit – touching ceremony.

At one point, Percy started to sniff. When I handed him a tissue, he took my hand and whispered, 'We should do this, you know.'

I snorted with suppressed laughter and he seemed affronted. I sincerely hoped he'd been joking.

After the church service, guests were transported to the Blenheim Hotel on Marine Parade. The windows of the dining room were open, and the cry of gulls could be heard as we tucked into fresh crab and lobster.

After the wedding breakfast, Elijah stood to make a speech. I didn't envy him the task. What could he say about two people who'd both been widowed and had met in the intelligence corps during the war? I expected him to mumble a few words of congratulation, read out the telegrams, and then sit down and light a cigarette.

Instead, he spoke movingly about finding love in later life, based not on youthful infatuation but on friendship, companionship and acceptance. I saw Horace dab a handkerchief to his eyes. I was glad he and Elijah had found the same happiness as my father and Katherine but felt sad that no declarations of their love could ever be made in public. They made the best of what they had with quiet dignity.

I was quite teary-eyed by the time Elijah sat down, and Percy was almost blubbing. I practically had to carry him onto the ballroom floor when my father and Katherine invited other guests to join them for their first dance.

After he'd danced with Katherine, my father came and took my hand, and I felt my eyes fill up once again. I couldn't remember when we'd last danced together, but I knew it was a long time ago, when my mother had still been alive.

'As strange as this may sound,' he said, 'I wish your mother was here today. She would be very proud of you.'

I blinked back tears. 'She'd be happy that you've found Katherine.'

'Yes. I believe she would. She was always kind-hearted. It's one of the things I loved about her. I want you to know that I'll never forget her. A day doesn't go by without me thinking about her.'

'Me too.' I wished he'd said this to me years before. Of all occasions to say it, he chooses the day he gets married. But that was typical of my father. Timing was never his strong point. And I had to accept that instead of rebelling against it.

When the music ended, Father went to reclaim Katherine, and Percy was back by my side.

'Are you having a bit of a blub now?' he asked, putting his arm around my waist.

'Just a bit,' I admitted.

'You're happy for them, though, aren't you?'

'Of course.' We twirled at speed across the dance floor.

'Do you still plan to move in with Millicent and Ursula?'

'Yes, because I think it's the right thing to do. We'll get along better as a family if we're not all under the same roof.'

He glanced over to where my father and Katherine were dancing, their faces almost touching.

'I can see your point,' he acknowledged.

After our dance finished, Percy stole Millicent from the arms of my grandfather and started to spin her around the floor. Gramps happily retired to the lounge with Nan for a reviving cup of tea.

Mrs Siddons caught my eye, and I went over to sit next to her by the side of the dance floor. She was resplendent in pale green silk and a matching silk cap. The string of jade beads around her neck would have Emerald spitting with envy.

'Have you enjoyed your holiday, my dear?' She held up a pair of old-fashioned lorgnette spectacles and peered at me. I wasn't sure if they were an affectation or if she used them to avoid wearing glasses. 'I hope you haven't been bored.'

'Not at all,' I replied. 'Devon has been fascinating.'

'Have you been able to spend any time with Katherine? She really is a most interesting woman when you get to know her.'

And you don't know the half of it, I thought.

'I feel I know her a little better,' I said. 'Although there's still a lot I'd like to talk to her about.'

'Good. I'm pleased to hear it. And I'm glad to see you looking so well. I have a feeling I'm going to need your energy in the coming months. Are you still planning to move in with Millicent and Ursula?'

I nodded, watching Bea shyly accept Percy's hand for the next dance while her brother offered his to Millicent.

'Good. You three will make a formidable campaign team.'

I switched my attention back to Mrs Siddons. 'You think Baldwin will call an election?'

After Prime Minster Andrew Bonar Law had fallen ill earlier in the year, he'd been replaced by Stanley Baldwin. The newspapers were predicting a winter general election.

'It's likely.' She sighed. 'The Matrimonial Clauses Act has been given royal assent, so at least I helped to achieve something. I could get booted out this time round.'

This made me think of the conversation I'd had with Nathalie and Annette regarding the change in divorce laws – just before I'd told Mrs Green about the silver ring on the dead man's finger. What would have happened if I hadn't mentioned it? They'd never have known the truth about Ferdinand and perhaps Nathalie would have divorced Rupert and gone to London with Emile. Maybe Rupert would have lost Smugglers Haunt to his creditors and sought drunken solace in the arms of Emerald.

'What are you thinking?'

I roused myself from my thoughts and found Mrs Siddons scrutinising me through her lorgnette spectacles again.

'What ifs,' I replied.

'It rarely pays to dwell on what could have happened,' she said firmly.

This was true. Even if I'd never mentioned the ring, Nathalie, Emile, Marc or Annette might one day have discovered more about the fate of their beloved Ferdinand. Secrets had a way of revealing themselves even without the help of nosy journalists.

'I can't help thinking about what might have...'

She cut me off. 'You're too young for what ifs and might haves, because you still have time to put everything right.' To my surprise, she glanced over at Percy when she said this.

Seeing her look, he bounded over to her side and held out his hand. 'Would the honourable member of parliament do me the honour?' He gave a low bow.

Mrs Siddons didn't need any persuading and allowed herself to be escorted on to the dance floor.

For a few moments, I watched them glide regally to a slow waltz, then decided it was time to confront my boss. Elijah's reluctance to discuss when he and my father had first met Katherine made sense now. He'd never talked to me about their time in the intelligence corps, however, I suspected he had shared details of his exploits with Horace.

I found the pair of them seated in the lounge, large glasses of brandy in hand.

Without preamble, I flopped down into the chair next to Elijah and said, 'When were you planning on telling me my stepmother was a spy?'

Horace smiled.

'Have you heard of the Official Secrets Act 1911?' Elijah responded. 'You may find this hard to believe, but it means not telling state secrets to nosy parkers like you.'

'Did you or my father ever go undercover in occupied territory?' I hoped the emotion of the day and the alcohol of the night might make him more talkative on this subject than usual.

Elijah rolled his eyes. 'The Act was extensively revised in 1920 to include a paragraph specifying that on no account should you trust Iris Woodmore with state secrets.'

Horace chuckled, lit a cigar, and passed it to Elijah.

'You must have undertaken some difficult missions,' I persisted.

Elijah leant back and puffed on the cigar, regarding me with exasperation. 'Do you know the toughest thing I've ever had to do?'

'No, what?' I asked eagerly.

'Keep you out of trouble.'

34

'Where are you going?' Percy asked.

We'd taken a last stroll at Coryton Cove before returning to the Jewel of the Sea, where Emerald was throwing an impromptu party for our last night. The following day, Millicent and I would catch the train to Walden, and Percy was motoring back to London. Mr Andrews and Dame Cicely would also be leaving as the Theatre Royal's run of *The Second Mrs Tanqueray* had come to an end the previous night.

I had a feeling the lure of smuggled brandy and sitting up with theatricals would bring Percy back to the Jewel of the Sea boarding house in the future.

I glanced at my watch and put my cocktail down on the bar. I'd only taken a few sips, uncertain as to what Emerald had put in it. 'I won't be long. I'm just going for a short walk.'

'Are you going to see Emile?' Percy sipped his drink, trying to appear unconcerned and not succeeding.

I didn't reply. As I slipped out of lounge, I noticed Millicent shrug and Percy roll his eyes.

The sun was low in the sky, though there was still plenty of light. I enjoyed the stroll to Boat Cove, however, the steps to Lea Mount were more challenging. Once I was on Teignmouth Road, I regained my breath and hoped I didn't look too sweaty.

Smugglers Haunt was closed up and I made my way through the garden, stopping to inhale the rich scent of the Ferdinand Pichard roses.

I felt a flicker of trepidation although I knew the figure I could see strolling across the beach below wasn't the ghost of Dick Endicott searching for his missing treasure. I took a deep breath and walked through the tiered garden and down the slope to Smugglers Cove.

I crossed the beach and joined Marc at the foot of the cliff. He stood by the entrance to the cave, looking as tired as he had the previous day. He'd made a brief appearance at the wedding reception to wish the happy couple well. Annette hadn't been with him.

That morning, I'd come across a slip of paper in my purse. I guessed he'd put it there when I was dancing with Percy. Scrawled on it were the words;

8 p.m. at the cave

followed by the initial *M*. I'd known immediately who it was from.

'I can't believe Ferdinand was here all that time.'

'I'm sorry.' I peered into the cave. It looked nothing like it had three weeks ago when we'd found the skeletal remains.

Marc turned to face me. 'Not the most romantic place to meet, is it? But then neither was the water tower, I suppose.'

I smiled at the memory.

'I wanted to come here one last time before we leave. To say goodbye to Ferdinand.' He reached out to take my hand. 'And to see you. I'm sorry we haven't had the chance to be alone together these last few weeks. Every time I've tried to find you, you've had your friends around.'

'That's probably just as well.' I remembered the last time we'd been alone together.

Five years ago, we'd huddled inside the entrance to the water tower of the Park Fever Hospital. On a miserable day, with rain sweeping across the lawn, I'd covered my head with a raincoat and ran to the water tower, hoping no one had seen me.

Marc was due to leave that morning. Despite the guilt we both felt about Annette, we couldn't resist one more kiss before we said goodbye. Goodbye forever. Or so I'd imagined at the time.

'I've thought about you often. I want to apologise for the way I behaved back then. You were young, and I...' He bowed his head. 'I should have known better. I shouldn't have become involved with you the way I did.'

I studied his serious face – the dark lashes over intense eyes and the upturned corners of his lips. When the two men had walked through the doors of the hospital and the other volunteers had gazed admiringly at Emile, something had drawn me to Marc. It was the clearness of his eyes, the purpose of his walk. He gave the appearance of being someone who had all the answers. Someone who could solve all your problems. And more than anything, I'd wanted that.

I shrugged. 'A few kisses? I was glad of them.'

He gave a rueful smile. 'You were so unhappy when we met. And older than your years. You'd seen so much.'

And even more was to come. I thought of the horrors of the military hospital that had lain ahead.

When I'd met Marc, I'd just turned eighteen and was still recovering from my mother's death three years earlier. Whenever grief or fatigue threatened to overwhelm me, I'd run and hide in the water tower. One evening, Marc had been exploring the grounds and found me there. It became our secret meeting place. A few snatched moments away from the real world.

As I got to know him, I discovered he was as lost as everyone else at that time, living with the uncertainty of war. He told me about his life in Belgium, how he'd been studying for his law degree when Germany invaded. And why he'd decided to marry Annette and make sure she got away safely before he and his friends joined the resistance. In turn, he'd wanted to know all about my life.

At first, we simply shared our stories. Then, one day, we shared a kiss. Our secret meetings became more frequent after that.

He gazed at me sadly. 'I was older than you and should have behaved more responsibly.'

'I think you were tired of being the responsible one.' He'd only been twenty-four then, yet he'd taken on the burden of caring not just for his family but for the Vandammes and Annette. I'd sensed his longing for some respite from it all.

'Getting out of Belgium with Emile wasn't easy. He nearly got us arrested several times,' he admitted. 'Before that, I'd looked after Annette, Ferdinand and their uncle. If it hadn't been for the war, I'm not sure Annette and I would have married. I loved her and wanted to protect her... but, in different circumstances, the relationship would probably have run its course as we grew up.' He shrugged. 'There's no point in dwelling on that now. She relies on me, and it's not a bad marriage.'

'Are you happy?' I couldn't help but ask.

'Coming to this country has given me many opportunities. And I've met some wonderful people, like your grandparents and Stephen and Gwen. Moving to London will give me more challenges. I hope more fulfilment. It's an exciting new chapter for us.'

It was an answer of sorts, and I didn't push him further. 'I hope it works out for you.'

'And you? I hope your life is what you want it to be. I was afraid, looking back, that I'd added to your unhappiness.'

I shook my head. 'You made me feel alive. You gave me hope for the future and for a relationship.'

He seemed puzzled. He'd never made a secret of the fact that he was married.

I smiled and corrected myself. 'Not of a relationship with you. Of the possibility of future relationships. That there could be excitement in my life, adventure and possibly, one day, love.'

'I wish you all of those things. Perhaps you've already found them? You have a loving family and good friends. Maybe Percy is more than just a friend?' He tilted his head to one side and scrutinised me.

'Percy's just a friend. I'm lucky to have him and Millicent in my life.' I thought of my other friends. Ben Gilbert, Mrs Siddons, and Elijah and Horace, my two hard-drinking guardian angels. And my family, which up until recently had consisted of my father and Lizzy. I'd also had my share of losses. First my mother and then my oldest and dearest friend. How I wished I could have them both back. But Mrs Siddons was right. There was no point in what ifs. 'And I've recently gained a stepmother.'

He smiled. 'Katherine is a good woman. I think she and your father will be very happy together.' He took my arm. 'It's getting dark, we should get back.'

It was strange to walk along a beach at sunset arm-in-arm with the man I'd shared my first kiss with.

'Did Superintendent Endicott believe Nathalie's story?' I couldn't stop myself from asking.

He nodded. 'Mrs Challacombe confirmed she recognised the photograph of Ferdinand as Jean Claes. And thanks to you and

Stephen, we have Harriet Green's testimony. I hope the court will be lenient on Nathalie and understand she acted impulsively on discovering what Rupert had done.' He paused. 'I hope you'll be lenient too.'

I got the message. 'Nathalie's defence will be that she never meant to kill Rupert. You want me to forget everything I heard her say.'

And not mention Annette's part in Rupert's death were the unspoken words that hung in the air.

'There's no reason for you to be involved any more. Superintendent Endicott is satisfied with the information he has. Nathalie has confessed to pouring the chloral hydrate into Rupert's drink.'

I refrained from saying that she'd been able to do this without being seen because Annette had suggested we all go out to the terrace – and that I also suspected she'd created a diversion at the doctor's house to enable Nathalie to steal the drug in the first place. But that was merely supposition – I had no proof.

'Don't worry. I'm leaving tomorrow. I have no intention of having further dealings with Superintendent Endicott or any other members of the Devonshire Constabulary if I can help it.'

He smiled. 'Thank you.'

We climbed the slope to Smugglers Haunt and went through the garden to the drive where Marc's car was parked.

He turned to gaze at the house. 'Soon this will be Katherine's. Do you think you will come back here?'

I thought of my grandparents. And my new friends, the Damerells. 'Yes. I think I might.'

'Good. It's a special house, and I think it can be a happy place again.'

'Will you come back?' I asked.

He shook his head. 'I need to take Annette away from Devon.

We have to make a fresh start.' He hesitated, then gestured towards the house. 'She regrets what happened here.'

I understood the meaning behind his words. 'I wish you both well.' My voice faltered slightly as I said, 'Goodbye, Marc.'

He was silent, making no move to get into his car. Then he reached out and took my hand. 'When I'm settled in London, do you think perhaps we could meet occasionally?'

'I'd like that.' I said the words quickly, knowing for that precise reason it would be wrong to see him again.

AUTHOR'S NOTE

In 1923, the year the events of this novel took place, my great-grandfather, Albert Salter, worked as an engine driver based at Exmouth Junction in Exeter. For many years, he drove a steam train from Exeter to Exmouth, once stopping the train and hopping down from the footplate to go and pick mushrooms in a nearby field – much to the annoyance of his passengers!

In 1923, Albert's sons, Lionel and Harold, attended Ladysmith Infant School with their friend, Clifford Bastin. While Clifford went on to find fame as a footballer for England and Arsenal, Harold, my grandfather, left school to work at the local branch of Lloyd Maunder, the butchers, before joining his father at Southern Railway.

When Arsenal reached the Cup Final in 1936, Clifford sent his old school friends tickets for the match. Lionel and Harold travelled up to Wembley to watch Clifford play for a victorious Arsenal.

After the match, Lionel took Harold to the famous Lyons Corner House on the Strand to meet his girlfriend, Louisa, who worked in admin there. Louisa introduced Harold to her sister,

Hilda, who was a Nippy at the Corner House. (Lyons waitresses were nicknamed Nippys due to the way they nipped between tables at speed.)

Two years later, Harold transferred from Exeter to London and married Hilda, my grandmother, in 1938. They were married for over fifty years. Lionel married Louisa in 1939. Sadly, Lionel died in 1942.

For many years, Harold and Hilda lived in Hither Green, opposite the Park Fever Hospital. Family holidays were spent in Dawlish, and this continues to the present day.

ACKNOWLEDGMENTS

I'd like to thank the following people for their continued support: my parents, Ken and Barbara Salter – my father particularly enjoyed his role as historical researcher for this novel; Jeanette Quay for acting as sounding board and filmmaker; and Barbara Daniel for editorial advice and encouragement.

Thanks to my editor, Emily Yau, and all the other brilliant members of the Boldwood Books team.

As ever, I'm indebted to the numerous people, books, libraries, museums and archives that contributed to my knowledge of this period. The British Newspaper Archive, the Friends of Higher Cemetery in Exeter, and the Royal Albert Memorial Museum in Exeter were especially helpful in the writing of this book.

MORE FROM MICHELLE SALTER

We hope you enjoyed reading *A Killing at Smugglers Cove*. If you did, please leave a review.

If you'd like to gift a copy, this book is also available as an ebook, hardback, paperback, digital audio download and audiobook CD.

Sign up to Michelle Salter's mailing list for news, competitions and updates on future books.

https://bit.ly/MichelleSalterNews

Explore the rest of Michelle Salter's gripping Iris Woodmore series...

An Iris Woodmore Mystery
DEATH AT CROOKHAM HALL
MICHELLE SALTER

An Iris Woodmore Mystery
MURDER AT WALDENMERE LAKE
MICHELLE SALTER

An Iris Woodmore Mystery
THE BODY AT CARNIVAL BRIDGE
MICHELLE SALTER

An Iris Woodmore Mystery
A KILLING AT SMUGGLERS COVE
MICHELLE SALTER

ABOUT THE AUTHOR

Michelle Salter writes historical cosy crime set in Hampshire, where she lives, and inspired by real-life events in 1920s Britain. Her Iris Woodmore series draws on an interest in the aftermath of the Great War and the suffragette movement.

Visit Michelle's Website:

https://www.michellesalter.com

Follow Michelle on social media:

twitter.com/MichelleASalter
facebook.com/MichelleSalterWriter
instagram.com/michellesalter_writer
bookbub.com/authors/michelle-salter

Poison & Pens

POISON & PENS IS THE HOME OF
COZY MYSTERIES SO POUR YOURSELF
A CUP OF TEA & GET SLEUTHING!

DISCOVER PAGE-TURNING NOVELS FROM
YOUR FAVOURITE AUTHORS &
MEET NEW FRIENDS

JOIN OUR
FACEBOOK GROUP

BIT.LYPOISONANDPENSFB

SIGN UP TO OUR
NEWSLETTER

BIT.LY/POISONANDPENSNEWS

Boldwood

Boldwood Books is an award-winning fiction publishing company seeking out the best stories from around the world.

Find out more at www.boldwoodbooks.com

Join our reader community for brilliant books, competitions and offers!

Follow us
@BoldwoodBooks
@BookandTonic

Sign up to our weekly deals newsletter

https://bit.ly/BoldwoodBNewsletter